Dear Readers:

I hope that you will enjoy reading *Shades of Desire* as much as I enjoyed creating Jazz and Jeremy's world. All writers hope that their work will touch the lives of their readers. That's especially true because for me because *Shades of Desire* portrays a dilemma that many women face—finding love with someone society says is "wrong."

I wrote *Shades of Desire* because I wanted to take a very honest and realistic look at interracial dating. Jeremy and Jasmine have found everything they'd hoped for in one another. Unfortunately, though their hearts and minds were one, their families and friends were divided. Jazz and Jeremy must face some difficult truths, and I hope after reading *Shades of Desire* you'll be willing to examine some secret places in your own heart and discover what true love is really all about.

All of One World / Ballantine's Indigo Love Stories prove that love comes in many shades. I'm so happy to be a part of this wonderful series of stories written for us by women like us.

Best wishes,

Monica

Published by Ballantine Books:

BREEZE by Robin Allen
DARK STORM RISING by Chinelu Moore
EVERLASTIN' LOVE by Gay G. Gunn
LOVE'S DECEPTIONS by Charlene A. Berry
SHADES OF DESIRE by Monica White
WHISPERS IN THE SAND by LaFlorya Gauthier
LOVE UNVEILED by Gloria Greene
CARELESS WHISPERS by Rochelle Alers

SHADES OF DESIRE

Monica White

One World

THE BALLANTINE PUBLISHING GROUP • NEW YORK

Ballantine Books
Published by The Ballantine Publishing Group
Copyright © 1996 by Monica White
Excerpt from *Whispers in the Sand* copyright © 1996 by LaFlorya Gauthier

http://www.randomhouse.com

Library of Congress Catalog Card Number: 97-97087

This edition published by arrangement with The Genesis Press, Inc.

ISBN: 0-345-42218-X

Manufactured in the United States of America

First Ballantine Books Edition: May 1998

10 9 8 7 6 5 4 3 2 1

Acknowledgments

I would like to thank my fiancé Richard Volz for being there for me. You gave me support and you believed in me from the beginning to the end of this book when no one else would.

Thank you Pat Matznick, Debbie Hughes, and Melissa Payne for being critics and good friends.

Last, but not least, thank you Wilbur and Dorothy Colom for your infinite patience when I had so many questions.

SHADES OF DESIRE

Chapter One

IT WAS MY twenty-sixth birthday. To celebrate, I was going out with my girlfriends—I hadn't had a date in months, and it was killing me!

Taylor, my roommate and best friend, had actually agreed to go with us, giving up her beloved Cameron for one night, just to be nice to me. I like Cameron and can understand what Taylor sees in him. The only problem is, he's white. Taylor says she doesn't care, that the problems black woman/white man relationships cause are a small price to pay for love. But personally, I didn't think I could do it.

"Jasmine, you about ready?" Taylor stood at the door to my bedroom, watching me put on my lipstick. "Danielle called. She and Simone are on their way."

"How about you?" I asked. "You're not even dressed. If it were Cameron, you'd be ready."

She smiled. "If it were Cameron, I wouldn't be wearing anything at all."

I felt a flash of jealousy. "I can't believe you're giving him up for tonight."

"For you . . ." She let the thought go unexpressed. "Besides, there's nothing wrong with wanting to spend all my time with Cameron. When you find the right man, you'll see." She walked out of my room to finish dressing.

I looked at myself in the mirror. I had spent a lot of money on a birthday gift for myself: a dark, mustard-colored dress, cut in a V that highlighted my full breasts and caramel complexion. Maybe I'll get lucky tonight, I thought. My hair looked good, cut shorter than I had ever worn it (the women at First Federal would be knocked out tomorrow when they saw me), and my makeup was done to perfection, making my brown eyes seem dark, even sultry.

I shouldn't have broken up with Reggie, I told myself, then realized with a stab of anger that it had been the only thing to do. He had been screwing around with every skirt in town, and when he got Anita pregnant, that was it. Still, the thought of him inside me, his hands on my breasts, quickened my breathing beyond control and I was glad the doorbell rang to distract me.

"Where's the birthday girl?" Danielle asked. I walked out of my room to greet her.

"You look great!" she said. "New dress?"

"I call it the man-catcher," I told her. "If it doesn't work, I'll ask for my money back."

Danielle was the wildest of our group; she knew the best places in town. "We're going to the Catnip

Club," she announced. "Some friends at work were talking about it. They say the music's out of this world."

"Where's Simone?" Taylor asked, joining us and kissing Danielle hello.

"She's meeting us at the club. Come on. We'll take my car."

The club looked like a small house from the outside. We pulled into the parking lot. "Intimate," I said.

Danielle smiled. "You won't be disappointed."

We got out of the car and walked to the front entrance. A doorman checked our IDs and we entered a courtyard where there was a wading pool with a small fountain and a bar. There was a bunch of people, both black and white, dancing in the fresh air; the music from inside blared from speakers on the eaves. It sounded wonderful. I couldn't wait to get on the dance floor.

"Let's go in," Danielle said, leading the way. Simone was already waiting for us inside. We hugged and kissed one another in greeting. Taylor was the only one of the group with a permanent man; Simone and Danielle, like me, were cruising.

The dance floor was already crowded. Confetti sprayed from the ceiling and fog drifted from the floor. The music—jazz, my favorite—was amplified from ten-foot speakers scattered around the sides of the floor. Couples were dancing on top of all of the speakers.

We got drinks at the bar. Almost immediately, a great looking guy asked Danielle to dance, so I carried her glass back to a table. "It's *my* birthday," I muttered.

"You've got to be more aggressive," Simone said. "Look at that guy on the speaker. I think he's cute. I'm going to ask if I can dance on the speaker with him."

"Girl, are you crazy? What if you fall?"

She laughed. "He'll have to catch me."

She walked over to him. He bent down when he saw her coming and helped her up. I couldn't believe her brazenness, and said so.

"While we're standing around, at least Simone and Danielle are dancing," Taylor replied.

Out of the corner of my eye, I saw a nice looking, older black man walk into the club. He stood for a moment, scanning the crowd, then caught my look and sauntered toward us.

"There's a man I could take home to mother," I said, hoping he would ask me to dance.

"He's cute," Taylor agreed. "But you know me."

"Yeah," I said, "Cameron and only Cameron."

He was approaching. I could feel my heartbeat quicken. He was gorgeous! Six feet tall, the body of an athlete, smooth, chocolate complexion, deep brown eyes.

"Would you care to dance?" he asked in a sensual voice.

I could only nod. He took my hand, leading me to the dance floor; I could feel his heat.

"I'm a little rusty," he whispered.

Rusty? The guy was a klutz! I couldn't believe someone so beautiful could not dance.

6

He stepped on my toes once, and then again. My brand-new shoes! I tried to smile and prayed that the song would end. When it did, I walked off the floor and he followed.

"That was great!" he said. "How about the next dance?"

"I'm really thirsty," I told him. The least he could do was buy me a drink.

"I'll find you again when they play something slow," he said, ignoring the hint.

Not if I see you first, I thought, turning away. The cheap bastard.

Simone was still up on the speaker, her arms around her partner's neck. She was a quiet, pretty, light-skinned girl, studying nights to be a nurse. She didn't have a chance to go out much, so she was obviously making the most of it.

"Did you get his number?" Taylor asked, coming up and handing me my drink.

"Are you out of your mind? Did you see the way he danced? And he wouldn't even buy me a drink. I don't care if he's the greatest stud since Denzel Washington."

Taylor laughed that throaty laugh of hers and threw her head back. Her shoulder-length black hair fell away from her face, revealing her olive complexion and intense eyes. No wonder Cameron was attracted to her. There was not a man in the world who would not have found her beautiful.

"I hope you won't mind," she said, "but I called Cameron. I was feeling lonely here, with the three of you dancing. He said he'd be here as soon as he could."

"He won't feel out of place?"

"I don't think so. There are plenty of white men here. White girls, too."

Taylor had met Cameron at the insurance company where they worked. She was a claims examiner, he an actuary. At first, the fact that he was white bothered me and most of her other friends. But they had been going together for almost a year, and now we accepted him. I knew Cameron's parents were unhappy that Taylor was black, but despite our closeness she did not confide her feelings about them to me. It was a problem we all pretended did not exist.

I smiled at her. "I'm glad he's coming. I felt guilty not inviting him in the first place."

"Whew, it's hot." Danielle joined us. The man she had danced with was nowhere to be seen. "I saw you out there, Jasmine. Where's your friend?"

"Same place yours is."

Danielle laughed. "Yeah. Men are scum. But hey, you gotta keep trying."

I knew Danielle always would. She worked as an assistant editor at a black magazine. Her aggressiveness got her promoted quickly, but it seemed to eventually turn off her boyfriends. She'd had dozens of affairs, none lasting more than three months. It suited her fine, she said, but I think she wanted one man, just like I did.

A deep voice asked me to dance. I turned around

to say no, thinking it was the guy who had first approached me. Luckily, the word stuck in my throat.

Standing before me was the most beautiful man I had ever seen. I figured him to be thirty, four years older than I, but he had the smooth skin of a schoolboy. He wore blue jeans and a jeans jacket, but I could tell he was heavily muscled—he works out, I thought. I looked at his legs: perfection. Just above them—I could only guess—but a telltale bulge made me yearn to know more. He seemed slightly shy, self-conscious, and I liked that. If he knew how gorgeous he was, it hadn't made him arrogant.

He looked at me with friendly green eyes. But he's white. Before I could think at all, I said, "Yes, I'd love to," and I was out on the floor, in his arms, letting myself melt against him.

"What's you name?" he whispered.

"Jasmine Smith. And yours?"

"Jeremy Collins. Is it okay if I call you Jazz? It's my favorite kind of music."

Jeremy. A white man's name. I knew no one named Jeremy. So what? I thought. Now I did. "Jazz is my favorite music, too."

"You dance wonderfully," he said.

"You, too."

"Do you work?"

"Yes. At First Federal. I'm assistant manager, claims adjustment."

"I'm a freelancer. A writer. Articles and books. Have you heard of *Castro's Children*?"

"I'm afraid not." I was determined to find a copy.

"It's just out. My latest. About what will happen in Cuba after Castro dies."

The song ended. We stood awkwardly for a moment, not touching. "It's my birthday," I blurted suddenly, desperate not to let him go.

His smile produced crinkles at the corners of his eyes.

"Really! That calls for a drink."

He led me to the bar. Danielle and Taylor, seeing us approach, moved away and pretended not to know me. "Have you ever been here before?" he asked.

"No. It's the first time I've gone out in a while, as a matter of fact."

He handed me my drink. "I've been here before. I like racially mixed clubs. But this is the first time it's really been fun."

I wasn't sure whether it was because of me, but I welcomed the sound of it. We stood at the bar, nursing our drinks, talking mostly about our shared passion: jazz.

The music changed to a ballad, and he led me back onto the dance floor. He had a wonderful scent, and when he took me in his arms and caressed my lower back, I could feel my nipples tighten and I pressed against him, surprised at the openness of my response. He grew hard against me, but he said nothing and did not kiss me. When the song ended, we again moved apart.

"I'd like to introduce you to my friends," I said, a little out of breath.

"I'd be honored."

Danielle and Simone were standing at the bar, talking to each other. "You guys, this is Jeremy," I said.

He offered to buy them drinks, and they accepted. I felt a little jealous, I don't know why. He went to place their order.

"I can't believe it," Danielle said. "Granted, he's gorgeous, but I never thought you'd go over to the other side."

I couldn't tell how serious she was. Did she care? I remembered she had once made a joke about Cameron and Taylor, how no white man could satisfy a black woman, and I wondered whether she was prejudiced or just making fun of Taylor.

"First Taylor, now you. What's the world coming to?" Simone was obviously teasing.

"It's only a dance," I told them.

"Sure," Simone said. "But I saw you out there with him. Anything more, and it'd be X-rated. What if he asks you for your phone number? Will you give it to him?"

"Maybe I will and maybe I won't. I doubt if he'll ask, anyway." If he did ask, and I prayed he would, I knew the answer.

He came back with the drinks, and talked to my friends. Taylor came up with Cameron; if either was surprised by Jeremy's presence, it didn't show. Jeremy asked me if I wanted to dance again, and we went back on the floor. I was hoping they'd play another slow song, but the music was upbeat, and the sense of intimacy that had been so strong now vanished, leaving me unsure of what would happen.

"I've got to leave," Jeremy said. "An early interview tomorrow morning."

My disappointment must have showed, for he took my hand. "I had a really great time, Jeremy. Thanks for the drinks and for dancing with me. You made it a special birthday."

We walked off the dance floor hand-in-hand. "I'd like to see you again," he said. "Maybe we could go out for drinks or something."

He seemed suddenly shy. Is it because I'm black? I wondered. "I'd love to," I said, and we went to where Danielle and Simone were standing to borrow paper and a pen. I wrote down my number, and he gave me his.

"I'll call you tomorrow," he said. "Maybe we can do something tomorrow night."

Again, he seemed shy. "Yes, call," I said, hoping he would kiss me good-bye. But he merely squeezed my hand, waved, and disappeared into the crowd.

"I can't believe you gave him your number," Danielle said.

"So what? I was surprised he could dance." Now that Jeremy was gone, I wanted to go home. I saw the handsome black man out on the floor, trampling someone else, and I laughed. If I had continued to dance with him, I'd never have met Jeremy.

"Considering you've never been with a white man before, what did you think?" Danielle asked.

I kept my thoughts private. "I only danced with him. It was no big deal."

"Then take my advice," she said. "Don't make it one."

But I could still smell Jeremy's cologne and feel his hand on the small of my back.

Chapter Two

THE SUN STREAMING through the blinds woke me up. I'd slept past noon. I usually don't do that, but I'd had trouble falling asleep, thinking about Jeremy. I smiled to myself. The night had been amazing.

I could hear Taylor moving around in her room, and I knocked at her door. "What time did you get home last night?"

"This morning, really. We stayed at the club till it closed, then went back to Cameron's place." She opened the door and smiled at me. "Somehow we didn't get any sleep."

I thought of Jeremy. What would it be like to spend the night with him?

As if reading my thoughts, Taylor asked, "What did you think of Jeremy?"

"I liked him."

"He's sure good-looking."

"Yes, but he's more than that. He's—sweet."

"Think he'll call?"

"I don't know."

"If he does, are you ready for an affair with a white man?"

"Please. You sound like Danielle. Who said anything about an affair? All I did was dance with him."

"And give him your phone number. And look happier than at any time since you first met Reggie."

"I *was* happy," I admitted.

"Then my question stands."

"If you can do it, I can."

"It's not easy." Taylor stared at me intently. "On the outside, it may look okay, and God knows I love Cameron, but you're in for trouble, and you'd better go into it with your eyes open."

"What do you mean?"

"Take today, for example. Cameron and I are going to his parents' house for dinner. His brother Ben is coming back from Japan, and this will be our first meeting. I know his parents disapprove of me, but at least they've been polite. Ben has been stationed overseas for three years. I'm scared of what he'll think of me, how he'll react. Even Cameron admits Ben doesn't like it that I'm black. And Cameron looks up to Ben, always has."

She was close to tears. I put my arm around her. It was the first time she had ever spoken of her pain, and I felt it acutely. "When Ben meets you, he'll love you," I told her, but we both knew I could not promise it.

The phone rang. I ran to answer it. Jeremy!

"Hello," I said.

"Sorry to disappoint you," Danielle's voice said. "I gather from your breathlessness he hasn't called."

"Nope. No call. I didn't really expect one, anyway."

Okay, so I lied. "Never trust a man," Danielle said. "And particularly a white man. Want to go to the beach with me and Simone?"

It was better than sitting home waiting for the phone to ring. "Sure."

"What about Taylor?"

"She's off to see Cameron's parents."

"Then it'll be the three of us. Pick you up in an hour?"

"I'll be ready."

I hung up, packed my beach bag with a few essentials, and put on my bathing suit under shorts and a shirt. Then I called my parents; they were out, so I left a message on their machine. My parents live only an hour away, but I call them twice a week and try to visit at least twice a month. My brother Greg lives closer to them than I do, but ever since he married Patty three years ago, he doesn't have time for them anymore. It's Patty's fault; she's too possessive. She doesn't like him to spend time with anyone but her. He wants kids, I know, but she doesn't. He has a good job as an engineer, and they could travel if they wanted, but she only wants to be at home, making sure he's at her side like a puppy. The first time I met her, I told Greg I didn't trust her. He went back and told her what I said, and she's hated me ever since. I'll never forgive my brother for telling her.

I left a note for Taylor saying I'd gone to the

beach. I didn't want her to worry if I got back after she did.

I saw Jeremy's number on the piece of paper I had carefully placed on my dresser, and I was tempted to call him. What if he gave me the wrong number on purpose? When I was in high school, we used to do that to fend off the creeps. I picked up the phone, then put it down. What if he answered? I had no idea what I would say.

Danielle knocked at the front door. I grabbed my beach bag and made sure the answering machine was on. "It sure is hot," I said, greeting her.

"Florida weather," Danielle said. "Come on. Simone's waiting in the car."

I got in the backseat. "Hey, Simone."

She smiled. "Heard from Jeremy yet?"

"No, and I probably won't." I felt a stab of pain. "It's only been one day."

"Why not call him?"

"No way. He's supposed to call first. If he wants to talk to me, he knows how to reach me."

"This is the nineties, girl. It wouldn't kill you to call first."

"No way," I said again, proud and hurt and ashamed. They would never see how much I wanted him!

Clearwater Beach was packed, so we drove on to Venice Beach a little farther away. It was nearly isolated, and it didn't take long to find a perfect spot. We set out our towels and stripped to our suits. The sun was shining off the water, and there was a slight breeze. The sand was white, almost winter-white, and the water was deep green, the color of jade; if you looked far out, it turned to midnight blue.

I love Florida and wouldn't want to live anywhere else. But today, even with the sun and the breeze and the water, I felt restless, distracted, and I let my friends talk to each other while I thought about Jeremy.

Simone must have invaded my brain. "Does Jeremy have a brother?" she asked.

"I don't know. Why?"

"'Cause Jeremy's really cute. I thought there might be something in his genes."

"In his blue jeans," Danielle said, laughing. "Just wait till you have sex with him."

"Who said anything about sex? I don't think it'll go that far." But I had thought about sex with him, of course, wondering what it would be like with a white man. Different? More exciting?

"Is sex all you can think about?" I asked, censoring my own thoughts.

"Oral sex, as a matter of fact," Danielle said.

"Here we go," Simone said, smiling. "Please, don't tell us again how Billy made you come with his tongue." I wanted to hear it, and I know Simone did, too.

"You're just jealous," Danielle told her. "You've never had it done to you. But I think it's better than real sex, or at least as good."

"Oh, really? How so? To me there could be no comparison."

"How do you know if you've never experienced it? You've got to try it; it'll be the best thing that ever happened to you. But not just anyone can do it. He's got to have the right technique. I've been with a couple of guys that were chewing down there like they were eating a pork chop. But with Billy—ah, Billy, he could kiss and lick like he was tasting honey. The first time he did it to me I came so hard I damn near pulled his hair out."

"I wonder if Jeremy does it," I said, envisioning his mouth on my most sensitive spot. "Why do you think black men date white women?" I asked.

"It's a power thing," Simone said.

"For the sex," Danielle said simultaneously.

"What about black women and white men?"

"For the sex," Danielle said.

But Simone took the last question seriously. "For the experience, maybe," she said. "But I think it doesn't matter whether a man's black or white so long as he's considerate and kind, handsome and smart, and he likes you and you like him."

"Bravo!" Danielle said. "Only there's not a white man alive who's all those things."

"What about Cameron?" Simone asked.

"Taylor's in for a heartbreak."

What about *Jeremy*? I thought. But I didn't want Danielle's opinion. I wanted to find out for myself.

We swam and ate the picnic lunch Simone had brought. Soon, to my relief, it began to cloud over, and Danielle suggested we go home before the rain came. Usually I love the beach in the rain, with the water from the sky mixing with the water in the sea, but today I was anxious to get back to the answering machine, particularly after our conversation about sex.

It seemed to me it took forever for Danielle to drive home, and we dropped off Simone first. She wished me luck when she left us. "Let me know if Jeremy calls," she said, and I promised I would.

Danielle and I drove over to my house in silence. I was angry at her, not believing that she understood how deeply I felt about Jeremy, finding her prejudiced and shallow in her thoughts about white men. For all her sense of fun and all the good times I had with her, I wanted to be away from her influence.

In front of my house, I kissed her good-bye and thanked her, then, without looking back, raced up the stairs to my apartment.

Taylor was not yet home, so I went into my room to check the machine. One call. Jeremy? It had to be.

Relishing the anticipation, as though I were actually going to see him face-to-face at that moment, I went to the bathroom to shower, and put on my best jeans and a T-shirt. Then I walked slowly to the machine and pushed PLAY.

"Hi, Jas. It's Greg. Please give me a call when you get back."

My dumb brother, who never called unless he wanted something.

Mad at him for not being Jeremy, disappointed to my core, I debated not calling Greg back even as I picked up the phone and dialed. Patty answered.

"It's Jasmine. Is my brother there?" My voice, I knew, was cold. I really hated Patty. She didn't have a job, but she didn't do anything around the house. The one or two times I visited them it was a mess. Greg was a neat freak, and I wondered how he let her get away with it. Oh well, it was none of my business.

"Yes, he is," Patty said, then paused. I waited for her to call him to the phone, but she said nothing.

"May I speak with him, please?" I could feel my anger rise.

"Hold on." This time she dropped the phone on a table and screamed, "Greg!"

He got on the line. "Jasmine, how are you doing? We haven't talked in a long time."

Uh-oh. Charm. He must want something really big, I thought. "Come on, Greg. What's the deal here?" I was dying to get the conversation over with and drown my disappointment in a gin and tonic. The last thing I wanted was phone games with my brother.

"I need a favor. I know you've been working at the bank. Maybe you can pull some strings. Well, I need a loan."

"For what?" He was doing well, I knew. I didn't think money was a problem.

"Actually, the loan's for Patty. She wants a new car. I was hoping you could help us out."

A new car! For the number of times she got out of the house, she barely used the old one.

"Does she have a job yet?" I knew she didn't.

"Not exactly. But she's looking. That's why she needs the new car."

He sounded so pitiful it made me sick. He was her

slave! I couldn't understand what hold she had over him. Sex? Hell, she wasn't even pretty. Suddenly, I felt sorry for him.

"I'll see what I can do, Greg. But I can't make any promises. Give me a call at the office Monday morning and we'll try to set something up."

He was still my brother, and I loved him. In the long run, I would probably regret helping him, but I was going to do all that I could.

"Bless you, Jas," he said, then hung up.

Depressed and tired, I went to the kitchen to make myself that gin and tonic. *Damn!* No man. No sex. A brother in trouble. Parents getting old. A white man who fulfilled my expectations. This tonic is flat. I'm going to cry. I really am. I'm going to cry and cry and never stop crying.

The phone rang.

Chapter Three

I S JASMINE THERE?" an unfamiliar voice asked. Jeremy!

"This is she." I fought to keep my voice under control.

"Hi, this is Jeremy. You busy?"

Never too busy for you, I thought. No matter what. But all I said was, "Just fixing myself a bite to eat."

"I don't want to interrupt—"

"You're not interrupting anything. Actually, I'm having a drink before dinner."

He sighed. "That sounds good. I could use one myself. I was with this guy all day—you know, the Cuban informer. He's been in all the papers. I'm writing an article on him. That's why I couldn't call you sooner."

"You wouldn't have reached me," I said, cool as sherbert. "I spent the day at the beach with Danielle and Simone."

"Your friends? The women I met last night? I envy you."

"Yes. They're very attractive."

He laughed. "I don't mean that. I'm jealous you had the day off and I wasn't with you. Next time you go to the beach, I hope it's with me."

Drop your cool, I told myself. He really means it. "I went to the beach so I wouldn't sit by the phone," I admitted. "I wanted you to call. I *really* wanted it, but when you didn't—well, I had to take my mind off you."

There was a long pause. "So you felt it, too," he said at last.

"Felt what?"

"That something special happened last night. Something between us."

"Yes," I whispered, my skin on fire.

"I thought it was just my own fantasy. That you'd never go out with a white man, that all you wanted was a dance and good-bye."

"I wanted more. I still do."

"Then what about tomorrow? Dinner?"

I'd have cancelled a date with Wesley Snipes. "Dinner would be fine."

"I'll pick you up at seven. What's your address?"

"I don't want to give it to you."

"Then how can I—"

"If I tell you, you'll hang up. And I want to talk to you some more."

"If you give me your address, I'll talk as long as you like. If not—"

I told him.

We talked for two hours. It was as long as I've ever spoken to anybody on the phone, but it seemed to me like two minutes; I couldn't believe the time when we finally hung up.

We talked of ordinary things and special ones. He told me about his more exciting assignments; he really was an expert on Cuba, and he'd had some dangerous adventures there. I described Reggie and he swore he would never behave like that; he was really mad. We talked of religion, of our backgrounds, of high school and college. We talked about movies and food, our parents and siblings (he had only two sisters; tough luck, Simone!), the trips we had taken and the friends we had made. The only thing we didn't talk about was sex, but sex hung over our conversation like a sweet cloud, and there was no question that if he had been with me, we would have made love.

When we said good night, it was with the certainty that for us there would be a tomorrow. A tomorrow when he would hold me in his arms.

I went to bed before Taylor came home, only calling Danielle and Simone to tell them about Jeremy. Luckily, neither of them was home, so I was able to leave a message on their machines without having to go into details. I didn't want to talk to anybody. I only wanted to listen to his voice replayed in my blood.

I set my alarm so that I could get up early enough to go to church. I knew that Pastor Baldwin would be glad to see me; it had been a couple of weeks since my last visit.

When the alarm went off, I was already up and getting dressed. I enjoyed going to church, and on this hope-filled day I would especially enjoy listening to the choir. When I got to church, it felt like coming home. I was hugged and kissed and my friends told me they had missed me. I sat down in my usual spot and listened to the singing. As always, the music touched my soul and soon I was rocking back and forth like everyone else in the pews. When Pastor Baldwin stood up, I knew he was going to talk to me.

Indeed, his sermon was on prejudice. He spoke of how destructive it was, how hating a man because of his color was as silly as hating a tree because it shed its leaves. If others despised us because we were black, it was because they feared we would take away their jobs. But the antidote was not to hate them back. It was to try to understand them, to live alongside them, to recognize that there were good and bad whites just as there were good and bad blacks, that we had to seek out what was in the inner man, just as we had to find what was in ourselves, and to judge by that, not by color or accent or religion or political beliefs. We were, truly, all God's children, and if we loved God we could love his children as well, black or white, Muslim or Jew.

When the service ended, I went up to Pastor Baldwin to tell him how much I enjoyed his sermon. I wanted to say how relevant it was to me, but I became suddenly shy.

"It's been awhile since you've been here, and I'm glad that you came today," he said, hugging me.

"I love to hear you talk, and I love to listen to the choir."

"You should join."

"I will, when I find the time." I knew it was a lame excuse, but it was the truth.

"When are you going to bring a young man to church with you?" he asked.

I wasn't prepared for the question. "I guess when I find one."

"You will," he said. "God will see to it. Just be patient."

He was going to say more, but he had to greet other members of the congregation. I told him I'd be back the next Sunday.

When I got into my car, though, his question kept coming back. Could I bring Jeremy to an all-black church? Would the congregation really be able to accept him? Did they all believe Pastor Baldwin's words, or were there some who could never love a white man, never be his friend? And deep down, beyond the fact that I found him attractive and wanted to see him again, could I spend the rest of my life with a man who was not of my race or color?

Lord, oh Lord, Jas, I said to myself. One dance and one conversation and you're thinking of *marriage*?

Taylor was awake when I got home.

"How did it go last night?" I asked her.

She raised her worried face to look at me. "It was awful!"

"Oh, Taylor, why?"

"It's Cameron's brother. He couldn't stand me."

"How do you know? Did he say anything?"

"No, but he couldn't even pretend like his parents do. He kept talking about Japs and Gooks, and all the time he was looking at me. I got the feeling he meant me. A Jap. A Gook. A Nigger."

She started to cry, and I put my arms around her. "But Cameron loves you. He's the important one."

"He does love me, he does. And after dinner he told me how ashamed he felt, and how sorry he was that I had to listen to Ben talk that way. But he didn't say anything when Ben was talking. He didn't try to stop him. He just sat quietly, looking miserable." Her tears increased.

"I'm so sorry," I said, knowing that my sorrow was in some small measure for myself as well. Would I run into the same hostility? Would Jeremy's sisters treat me the way Cameron's brother treated Taylor?

"What are your plans today?" Taylor asked, making an effort to stop crying.

"Jeremy's taking me out to dinner."

She put her hand to her mouth as though to dam up the words ready to spring from it. All she said was, "I'm glad he called."

Taylor left to go to a late church service with Cameron. With eight hours to kill before Jeremy arrived, I did my nails and my hair, went for a walk in the sunshine, and tried not to think of the evening ahead.

Home again, I called my parents. This time my father answered.

"Where have you been?" I asked. "I've been trying to reach you all weekend."

"We've been at the church, addressing envelopes and making calls. You know they've started their fund-raising drive, and they need all the volunteer help they can get."

"I miss you," I told him. "You and Mom both. She okay?"

"She's fine. But she's gone to the store. She'll be sorry she missed your call."

"She could call back," I said, but I knew she wouldn't. It was my job to contact them.

"I'll give her all the news," he said.

The news. Should I tell them about Jeremy? At the thought, my heart gave a little lurch. Too soon.

"I spoke to Greg," I said.

"Yeah? You hear from him more than we do."

I told him about our conversation.

"He's your brother, but I wouldn't get involved with him. Since he married Patty, he's changed. Your mother's nearly frantic about it. We don't even know him anymore."

I knew how hurt he was, how close he and Greg had been. "I told him I couldn't promise him anything, but I'll try to help him this one last time."

"It's your choice," my father said. "Just make sure you don't get hurt."

I promised to visit them the next weekend, and asked Dad to give my love to my mother. I hung up feeling sad. Greg was a severe disappointment to them; I wished that there was something I could do about him.

At six o'clock I put an En Vogue tape in the player. I love En Vogue, and danced to the music as I got dressed. Now it was time to do my make-up. I put a little powder on, some foundation, a little red blush on my eyelids, along with a thin line of black eyeliner on my top lids. I don't have to wear mascara because my lashes are naturally long, but for Jeremy I did it anyway, figuring my eyes would look darker, deeper, more mysterious. To finish, I applied my deep red matte lipstick, then looked in the mirror and was pleased. Irresistible, I thought.

I put on my silver earrings and sprayed on my favorite perfume, *Vol au Vent*. My black dress had a plunging neck and back, hugging every curve I possess. Too daring? No. Perfect. I was out to attract him. And if he was the man I imagined him to be, he would be turned on, not put off, by my openness.

I slipped on my black mules and put my lipstick, wallet, and keys inside a small black-beaded purse. I checked my hair one more time, adjusted the dress to show a little more cleavage, switched off the En Vogue tape, and went to the window to await his arrival.

I had butterflies in my stomach and my mouth was dry. He pulled up in front of the building in a

Saab convertible, and I ran into the bathroom and sprayed some holder on my hair; I didn't want it flying all over the place.

He knocked on the door. I took a deep breath and opened it for him.

"Hi, Jeremy," I said, but the words barely made it out of my mouth. He was twice as gorgeous as I remembered! Tonight he was dressed in a gray suit with a blue-and-white striped shirt and a yellow tie; (he looked more like a prosperous business-man than a reporter), but the suit was cut to reveal his athletic body, and his movements were fluid, as they were on the dance floor. His chestnut hair was tousled from the wind, and his green eyes had fire in them.

He took my hand gravely, slightly uneasy, slightly shy, and kept it in his own for a little longer than necessary. I wanted his touch to remain forever, but I pulled away nervously. "Some wine?" I asked.

"Let's have a drink at the restaurant. You're so beautiful you should be seen in the daylight."

He preceded me downstairs. There were still two hours of sunlight left, and when we got outside the sun glistened in his hair.

He opened the car door for me, and watched me intently as I slid in. "You look sensational," he said. "That's an even more beautiful dress than you wore to the club." I loved the feel of the butter-soft leather on my skin, and I ran my hands across the dash-board. The car had a CD player, and he had taken out a Wynton Marsalis disc, which he picked up from his seat and put in the player as he got into the car.

"Marsalis is my favorite," I said. "How did you know?"

"Because he's my favorite, too."

We started off. "Where are we going?" I asked.

"To the marina. I know a little restaurant there. Great music, and on a night like this, we can hear it best on the patio."

We drove along the water; the sun danced off the waves. There were sailboats on the horizon. Jeremy drove carefully, intent on the road, and I secretly studied his profile, again amazed at the softness of his skin and the humor in his eyes. I wanted to kiss those eyes, then move my mouth down to his mouth, and my hand down on his body to his center, his sex. But I sat demurely still, listening to the music. There was time. Plenty of time.

He stopped in front of a restaurant off the main road, ushered me in, and asked for his table. The maitre d', who obviously knew Jeremy well, escorted us to the patio overlooking the beach. There was a table for two with a blue tablecloth, white candles, wineglasses, water glasses, and silver that sparkled in the twilight. He handed us menus.

"We'll have a drink first," Jeremy said. He looked at me. "Planter's Punch?"

I did not know what it was. "If you say so."

"Two Planter's Punches," Jeremy ordered from a

waitress, then, turning to me, reached his hand across the table to put it on top of mine.

I literally could not speak, and he did not seem to want to. We merely gazed at each other, as if we had known each other for centuries. The pleasure in our eyes said enough.

The waitress brought our drinks, and I took a sip of mine. It had a fruity taste, and I drank again.

Jeremy smiled. He had full lips. A white man with full lips, I thought idiotically. The most beautiful man in the world.

"Don't drink too fast," he said. "There's rum in there and it'll sneak up on you if you're not careful."

"It's delicious," I said, putting my glass down.

His gesture took in the entire restaurant. "So, what do you think?" he asked.

"I love it. I love the drink. I can't imagine a nicer place."

"Our place," he said softly. A combo began to play inside, the music wafting out to the patio. He was wearing the same cologne I had liked so much the night of the dance, and I noticed how delicate his hands were, with thin, long fingers I could practically feel on my body. I was dizzy with the thought of making love.

A waitress brought menus and we ordered dinner—shrimp appetizers and steaks for both of us. With the steak, he selected a bottle of red wine. Funny, I thought. The liquor is having no effect. It's Jeremy who's making me tipsy.

It grew dark. The night sky was ablaze with stars.

We shared a dessert, a chocolate mousse cake with whipped cream, passing the spoon back and forth between us like a kiss. The coffee was rich and strong. We each had a brandy. He paid the check. And yet we did not move, but simply sat looking at each other, knowing the night was ahead of us, both of us hungry for each other, but shy.

"Let's go for a walk on the beach," he said at last.

"I'm wearing high heels."

"Take them off."

I was afraid of spoiling my dress, of him ruining his suit, yet suddenly a walk on the beach seemed a splendid idea, the *only* idea. I followed him down the steps that led from the patio to the beach, and we sat on the bottom step while he took off his shoes and socks and rolled up his cuffs.

Then, hand in hand, we stepped onto the sand, still warm from the sun. Light from the restaurant illuminated the spot where we stood, and I picked up some brightly colored shells and showed them to Jeremy.

"When I was a little girl, my parents would take me to the beach. I used to collect shells. I had a big jar of them, hundreds and hundreds. I only threw them away when I went to college."

"You can start another collection," he said. "My parents have a beach house in Key West, and we can go there any time we want."

The idea should have thrilled me, and in a way it did. It also made me think of Taylor and her troubles with Cameron's family, and I took my hand out of his and turned to face him.

"I have to ask you a question," I said. He saw the concerned look in my eyes, and his own expression became troubled.

"Shoot."

"Have you ever dated a black woman before?"

"Once. Briefly. It never came to anything. She was scared, and I might have been, too. We broke up after a week or so."

"But you're not scared now? With me?"

"Not at all. It's funny, you know? At the dance, there were plenty of white women, but you were by far the most beautiful woman there and I never hesitated. And now I don't see you as a black woman at all, but just as a woman, an infinitely desirable woman."

He said the words unemotionally, as though not to frighten me by being too forward, but I could sense the heat behind them.

"What about you?" he asked. "Ever dated a white man?"

"No, but my roommate does. And it's trouble, Jeremy. As much as she loves him and he loves her, it's trouble."

"Because some people are bigots, some people are idiots, and some people can't stand it if you're different. Sure it's trouble, Jazz, for me as well as you, although, granted, more for you. There are a lot of your friends who won't like me because I'm white, a lot of mine who won't like you because you're black. Still, I don't know about you, but I feel something between us that's more important than

41

what anybody else thinks. It's their problem, not ours."

I thought of Danielle, of how she would disapprove. I thought of Taylor's warning. I thought of my own certainty that I could never date a white man. I thought of how difficult it would be to bring Jeremy to church. I thought of how awkward I would feel when I met his family. I thought of all those things, and then I looked at him in the starlight, his own eyes searching mine for an answer, and I said, "I feel just what you feel, Jeremy. This is more than special. Black and white, we are meant to be."

I was shivering. The wind started to pick up. He took off his jacket and wrapped it around me, then stood holding me close to him. I could feel his heart pound. I could feel him grow hard. I felt immeasurably excited, immeasurably secure. He put his finger under my chin and raised my face toward his, lightly touched my lips with his, and I responded, conscious of my nipples rising against his chest and of a sweet wetness below I had not felt since Reggie left.

He paused, gazing into my eyes, smiled a small smile, and kissed me deeply, running his tongue across my lips, then into my mouth. Wild with desire, I kissed him back, my hand in his hair drawing him down toward me. He pressed his lower body against mine, and I thought, I'm yours. Fully yours. You can have me if you want me.

But he pulled away, shaking his head, breathless

as a long-distance runner. "No," he said. "Not here. It's cold, we've no blanket. The first time we make love, I want it to be perfect."

It's perfect now, my heart screamed, but I knew he was right. And I knew the anticipation would only make the consummation keener. "As long as you promise," I said.

"Promise what?"

"Promise you'll make love to me."

I was amazed at my own audacity, and I kept my voice light to hide the extent of my excitement.

He took the question seriously. "There's nothing in the world I want to do besides make love to you. But you have to make a promise in return."

"Anything."

"Listen before you answer. When we make love, *if* we make love, I want it to be the beginning of a contract. I don't mean marriage or anything like that—it's far too soon to think of it. I mean that ours will be a real relationship, a deep and profound giving of ourselves to each other, not just with our bodies but with our hearts."

"Oh, Jeremy—"

"Don't say anything yet. Think about it. You yourself brought up the consequences. You're special, Jazz, and I don't want to think you're sleeping with me just to see what it feels like, an experience to catalogue. I want to make love with you because it's the start of a deeper love, a dangerous love, because all true love is dangerous."

He stopped speaking, and I looked out at the

ocean, watching the light from a rising moon cross the waves like a golden carpet. Could I make such a commitment? Could I give up the life I knew for a different, more dangerous one with Jeremy? I had met him only twice; was he a con artist? But if he was, it seemed a strange kind of con—*don't sleep with me, black girl.* If he were sincere, was I willing to follow him, to commit as deeply as he wanted?

He seemed to read my thoughts. "Let's make a date for next Saturday. I'll call you Friday night, and I want you to say one word to me, either yes or no. If it's yes, I'll pick you up on Saturday at seven, just as I did today, only you'll have made a commitment, in effect given me more than just that word. If it's no, I'll understand. There'll be no hard feelings, and you'll never hear from me again. Is it a deal?"

My lips were dry, and I had trouble speaking. "A deal," I said.

"Good. I'll take you home."

He pulled up in front of my apartment house and opened my door for me, ever the perfect gentleman. I got out and we walked hand in hand to the building. I unlocked the door, feeling a little sad. The evening was magical, and I wondered, no matter what my decision, if we could ever recapture that magic.

"Thank you, Jeremy," I said. "Thank you for everything." *Please kiss me again,* I thought.

He did, again touching my chin to raise my lips to his. "You're so beautiful," he whispered.

I pressed my body to his and wrapped my arms around his neck. He kissed my eyes, my ears, my neck, again my lips, then pulled away.

"Friday," he said, his voice husky.

I knew then what my answer would be.

Chapter Four

MY GOOD MOOD must have shown the next morning, for when I entered the bank my coworkers smiled at me, even though I barely said hello. It was difficult to do, but I plunged into work—Monday is often the busiest day.

At around eleven o'clock, I went into the break room and fixed myself some coffee. Brigitte, one of my coworkers, found me there.

"Good weekend, huh?"

"How can you tell?"

"You're like an electric bulb. Lit up."

"As a matter of fact, it was a great weekend. Friday was my birthday, and I went to the Catnip Club. I met a man—"

"The Catnip? Isn't that a white club?"

"Mixed."

"Then let me ask. The man: Is he white?"

I felt a rush of anger. "What business is it of yours?"

She smirked. "That's answer enough. Experiencing a little jungle fever, huh?"

I turned away. "At least I've got a man."

Unfortunately, I couldn't see the look on her face.

Greg never called; it worried me. I thought about calling him to see what had happened, but I decided not to. I really didn't want to help him with the loan—as a matter of policy, the bank discouraged, though did not forbid, giving loans to family members—'cause knowing Patty, we'd have trouble getting it back.

When I got home that night, I changed into a pair of shorts and a T-shirt, then fixed myself something to eat. There was a good movie on Showtime, so I was annoyed when the phone rang. It was Danielle.

"How'd it go?" she asked.

I had thought about how much to tell her and decided to leave out the details. "It went great. He's a sweet man, and I like him. He's a writer, particularly interested in Cubans."

"Them?" The way she said the word made me glad I had not told her more.

"Yes, Cubans. In case you haven't noticed, there are several in Florida."

"Did you make love?" she asked, ignoring my sarcasm.

"No."

"Didn't you want to?"

"We didn't have a chance. All we did was go out to dinner."

"Didn't he come on to you?"

"No."

"What's the matter? Couldn't he get it up for a black girl?"

I remembered his hardness, my longing, and kept silent.

"You going to see him again?"

"I haven't made up my mind."

"Has he asked you for another date?"

"Not yet." It was technically true.

"He won't," she said positively. "Not if he can't get it up."

To change the subject, and because I really liked her in spite of her crazy prejudices, I told her about Greg. She was not surprised.

"I'm with your father. Don't get involved in it." Good advice, I knew, but I resisted it.

"Want to do something this weekend?" she asked.

"I'm not sure."

"Waiting for that call from Jeremy?"

Waiting for my heart to be doubly sure. "Yes."

"Well, if I find some action, and it doesn't include you, don't say I didn't ask you first."

"I promise," I said, and hung up.

It was after ten, and I was in bed reading when Taylor knocked softly on my door. "Can I come in? I want to ask you something."

"Of course."

Her face was drawn, her eyes red. She had obviously been crying.

"Taylor! What's wrong?"

"Cameron and I have broken up."

"No! You've got to be joking. Why?"

"His family's forbidden him to see me again."

It was as though someone had stabbed a knife in my stomach. "And he's agreed with them?"

"Yes. He told me we'd only be unhappy if we kept on going out. He couldn't marry me, he said. He wasn't brave enough for that. So he wanted to end it now, not prolong something that could never finally be."

I went to her and we embraced. "Everything'll work out, you'll see," I said, trying to convince myself as much as Taylor. "He'll realize how much he loves you, and he'll come back."

"No," she sobbed. "He's right. It could never work out. We were so much in love we denied it all these months. But with his family hating me, especially Ben, he'd have to disown them, and I couldn't ask him to do that."

She cried on my shoulder like a small child. "Give him time," I said. "Maybe everything will change."

"How much time?" she said bitterly. "A month? A year?"

"I don't know," I admitted. "But he'll come around, I promise."

Her sobbing increased. "I love him, Jasmine. I don't know what I'll do if he doesn't come back."

"He will, Taylor. He will."

But she and I both knew that the chances were small.

That night, I couldn't sleep. The conversation with Taylor played over and over in my brain. What if Jeremy were like Cameron? What if we fell in love only to have it end in heartbreak? I saw how miserable Taylor was. I would experience the same misery, the same pain.

But why should Jeremy necessarily be like Cameron? His family wasn't Cameron's; I didn't even know them. And Jeremy was stronger than Cameron, I was sure of it. If he really loved me, and if his family rejected me, he would reject them—or would he? Was Danielle right in her appraisal of white men? If she was prejudiced, maybe there was cause for it.

The thoughts attacked like bees. I tried to swat them away, but they came back, stinging. At last dawn arrived, and I left my room to make some coffee.

Taylor was already up; she hadn't slept either. I did not want to talk about my own fears, and she had told me everything about Cameron, so we sat like zombies, sipping coffee, feeling awful.

Finally, Taylor sprang up. "I'll get to work early for a change. Anything's better than sitting here."

"Right," I said, heading for the shower.

When I got to the office, I sent Taylor a bunch of balloons to cheer her up, then I worked without stopping until the phone rang.

"Jasmine Smith. How may I help you?" I always hated my "official" voice.

"It's Greg. Sorry I didn't call you yesterday, but I got tied up. I'm calling to ask you for a favor."

"A new car for Patty. I know."

"Actually, that was just an excuse to call you. I didn't want to say the real reason in front of Patty."

Uh-oh. Trouble. "What is it?" I dreaded the answer.

"I want to know if you'd co-sign a loan for me."

"Me? A loan for what? What's going on, Greg?"

He hesitated. When he spoke, his voice was low. "I lost my job a couple of weeks ago. Patty doesn't know about it. Nobody does, except you."

I was stunned. "Did they lay you off? What happened? I thought they liked your work."

"They did. It wasn't my work."

"Then what?"

"There was this woman. Anita. A vice president. I was working for her, and she sort of came on to me."

I understood it all. "Oh, Greg. You didn't!"

"The boss found out about it. There's a strict rule against it. We were both fired."

"And Patty?"

"She doesn't know. She'd kill me."

What an idiot. My brother with the brains of a gnat. "I can't believe you'd jeopardize your marriage and your job for a lousy affair."

"I know. I know. Don't lecture me, Jasmine. I don't feel like hearing it. What I need to know is if you'll help me out or not. I'll get another job soon, but right now, we don't have any money to pay the bills." My head was spinning. I didn't know what to do. He didn't have a job and he was asking me to take a terrific risk for him. He was my brother, but if he were in my place and I in his, he'd never have done anything for me.

"I have to think about it," I said. "I'd be taking a

huge gamble if I co-signed. How could I be sure you'd ever pay it back?"

"You have my promise," he said.

"Fat lot of good that'd do if you can't get a job."

"Jasmine—"

"I've got to think about it," I said. "I can't give you an answer now."

"When will you decide?"

"Give me till the weekend. I'll call you on Sunday."

"Sunday's too late."

"Maybe you'll have a job by then," I said angrily. "That'll make the decision easier."

I hung up before he could say anything more. Almost immediately the phone rang again.

"Jasmine Smith. How may I help you?"

"Thanks for the balloons! They look great. Oh, Jasmine, it was so nice of you. I feel a million times happier," Taylor said.

And I felt a million times worse. I should have saved some balloons for myself, I thought. "You're welcome," I said, and burst into tears.

All in all, it was one of the worst weeks of my life. Every time I looked at Taylor, I thought of what a mistake I'd be making to say yes to Jeremy. Every time the phone rang, I thought it would be Greg.

Taylor quickly went back to being depressed. Living with her was like living with a cloud. Greg didn't call, but the papers were full of stories on rising unemployment, and I thought of him every time I read one. Yes, he was good at his job. But who'd want to hire someone who might screw around with his colleagues?

By Friday, I was a wreck. I barely got through the day, and almost decided to go to a movie just so I wouldn't have to answer Jeremy's call. Face the inevitable, I told myself. You've got to make up your mind.

I forced myself to stay at my desk after my coworkers had gone, needing a quiet place to be alone and think. Nothing made me any happier than I had been on Monday; I was obsessed both with Jeremy's kisses and Taylor's tears.

Finally, I went home. Taylor was in her room; I was sure I could hear her sobbing. I tiptoed past her closed door, hoping she wouldn't hear me, and closed my own door behind me.

I checked my machine. Good. No messages. He hadn't called yet. Maybe he never would. Maybe he had decided not to go on himself.

Then how would I feel? I asked myself. Miserable? Relieved? Both? And if relieved, would it be because he had made the decision for me?

Be a woman, I told myself sternly. Don't let anybody make up your mind for you.

Decide!

The phone rang. I let it ring three times, holding my hand on the receiver, my chest so tight I felt as if I had swallowed a fist.

Finally, I picked it up.

"It's Jeremy."

No, no, no, no, no, said my brain.

But my heart, and my voice, said, "Yes."

Chapter Five

HE ARRIVED PROMPTLY at seven wearing jeans and a green sport shirt open at the neck. He looked like a cowboy who had just washed up after a triumphant rodeo. I swear, not only his eyes and his mouth, but his entire body was smiling.

He hadn't told me where we were going, so I didn't know what to wear. I had chosen a fancy dress, like the one I had worn on our first date; now I wished I had settled for something less formal. I felt awkward, and not only because I had picked the wrong clothes, but because I was suddenly tongue-tied. This gorgeous man before me was a total stranger, I felt, and I had not the faintest idea of what to say to him.

"Aren't you going to kiss me hello?" he asked.

Yes. Of course!

We kissed lightly, tentatively, not with passion, but with the promise of passion to come.

"Where are we going?" I said.

"To the only place I know that's nicer than our restaurant."

"There couldn't be a nicer place," I told him.

"But there is. My home."

My expression must have been one of shock, for he added quickly, "Of course, if you'd rather go out—"

Out? Why, if we went to his house— I let the thought stay unfinished.

"I've bought steaks," he went on. "And a salad. Champagne. After all, this is a special celebration."

"Of what?"

"Of the fact your word was 'yes.' "

He was grinning at me, perfectly sure of what I would say.

"Your house is fine. And I can't think of a better reason for a celebration."

I shuddered as I said the words, a sexual tingle which seemed to rock my entire body. If he noticed, he did not say anything. Maybe he was shuddering himself.

In his car I told him about Taylor and Cameron. "It really affected me," I said. "You don't know how close I came to saying no."

He smiled. "I don't think I want to know."

"Seriously. It scares me so much."

"He's a pig," Jeremy said. "Why doesn't he just tell his brother to go to hell?"

"Is that what you'd do?"

"You bet I would! What's more important than love?"

Would you renounce your family for me? I wondered, but I did not ask. Would I renounce mine for someone I loved? Ah, it would never come to that. My family would support me, no matter what I did.

We were driving along a road on the outskirts of the city. I saw a mailbox that said Collins, and Jeremy turned just after we had passed it, steering along a dirt road overhung with tree branches. We came to a clearing, and his house loomed before us, a two-story structure from a hundred years ago, not very elaborate, but freshly painted white with dark green shutters and a red chimney. The fading sun danced gold off its windows. A driveway leading from the road we were on circled a freshly cut lawn edged with flowers, and Jeremy parked in front of the entrance and ran to my side to open my door.

"Welcome," he said. "May this be the first visit of many."

"It's lovely," I said. "You keep it beautifully."

"Actually, a gardener comes once a week to help out. But I love to putter, especially in the backyard. I've nearly an acre," he added with some pride, as though proclaiming an estate.

"It's very grand."

"I bought it years ago, when prices were way down. I'm not very rich, but the house is comfortable."

Not rich. Ah, well, one can't have everything. In fact, for some reason this pleased me. There would be race between us, but not money.

"Let's go inside," he said, and took my hand.

The entrance led to a hallway that divided the living room and dining room. There were, he told me, two bedrooms upstairs, one of which he had transformed into his study. "It gets the afternoon light," he said, "when I need it most."

We went into the living room. It had definitely been decorated by a man, thick furniture made more for comfort than looks, bookcases everywhere, prints on the walls advertising modern art shows. The most striking piece was the couch, large enough for four, leather back and cushions, bright blue and red throw pillows, a place to sit and to talk and, without discomfort, to make love.

"It's very private," he explained. "I can shut myself off from the world if I want to. But as you see, I'm close enough to town to go to a club every once in a while—if only to look for someone like you."

"No more clubs for you," I told him, "unless we go together."

"A deal," he said. "I loved dancing with you more than with anyone I've ever met."

"Let's dance now," I said, feeling a sudden surge of desire.

"No. Dinner first. Do you want a drink?"

"Didn't I hear someone say something about champagne?"

"I was going to save it for later," he said, "but if you insist—"

I was about to stop him, tell him anything would be fine, but he had bounded off to the kitchen and soon returned carrying a bottle wrapped in a towel and two champagne glasses, which he placed ceremoniously on the coffee table in front of the couch, and then, with a flourish, opened the bottle.

Jeremy poured, and we toasted each other, sitting together, holding hands on the couch. Soon, though, he sprang up. "Time for dinner," he said. "Want to keep me company?"

"I can help," I said. "I make a mean salad dressing."

"Excellent! Your salad dressing it will be."

He led me through the dining room to the kitchen, one of those old, wonderful rooms with a butcher block table in its center on which were already laid out the meat and salad greens.

"We don't want to eat too much," he said. "But there's dessert, too, for afterward."

Afterward. After making love. There was no question that was what he meant, and again I felt the heat of desire. Let's forget the entire meal, I thought, but he had obviously planned the whole evening beforehand, and I let myself be led into his fantasy. There would be endless time for love.

We ate sirloins, salad, and drank the rest of the champagne while sitting in the dining room on large wooden chairs set close together. He had turned out all the lights in the room, and we dined in the glow of candles.

I told him about Greg. I realized it wasn't very romantic, but I wanted to rid my head of any thoughts except those of him, and my worry about my brother was the only impediment.

When I finished, I had tears in my eyes. "I don't know what to do," I told him.

Jeremy listened with great seriousness. "Since you're his sister, I think you have to do something. You'll feel too guilty if you don't. But only co-sign for a certain amount. No more than you can afford to lose in case you're the one who has to pay the money back."

It was such a simple solution, yet I hadn't thought of it. I felt my mind clear, and his face and body came into sharp focus. "You're a genius."

He stood, and I stood with him. "And you're the most beautiful woman I've ever known."

He took me in his arms and kissed me, trailing his hands down my back and sides until they reached the soft curves of my buttocks. Then he drew me close, and I could feel his maleness start to grow, and with a whimper I reached down to touch him. Fire was burning within me. I felt like I was about to explode.

He pulled aside, but only to lead me to the couch in the living room, where he sat down and drew me down to his side. He kissed me again, his tongue entering my mouth and caressing my lips, and his hand touched my breast, just above the nipple, and began to stroke it, always coming near, but never touching the pleasure point.

I began to moan, and reached for his belt.

"First you," he said softly, and with trembling fingers undid the buttons on the back of my dress until he could pull it off my shoulders. It dropped to my waist, and he kissed me again, this time his fingers playing gently over my bra, caressing my nipples until they stood out like small stones beneath the material. He reached behind me to unhook the bra, and I hunched my shoulders, letting it fall to my lap.

"I want to look at you," he said, and he gently pushed my shoulders back so that I was sitting straight, my full breasts aching for his touch.

"Beautiful," he whispered, and bent to kiss them, first the right, then the left, letting his tongue play about my erect nipples, occasionally arousing them still further with soft bites until he could stand it no longer, and he buried his head between them, reveling in my flesh.

Then, going back to my mouth with his, he lay down on the couch, pulling me down alongside him. I rolled on top of him and, raising my upper body, unbuttoned his shirt and shucked it off, then lay on top of him so he could feel my breasts against his chest.

His warmth was amazing! We lay almost still, our tongues working with each other's. Then he pulled off my dress, panties, and stockings with a strength made tender by need. I unbuckled his belt, and he pushed me away only long enough to take off his pants and underpants, shoes and socks. He lay down beside me again, and we kissed, and he rubbed my breasts with his hands until they tingled. I reached for him, felt his hardness; he moved his hand down and found me soft and wet.

"You're amazing," he said. "I want you."

Wordlessly, I rolled on my back, he above me, and I opened my legs to give him access. He was in me immediately, hard as steel, thrusting in and out with measured strokes, telling me how beautiful I was, how excited I made him. He grew faster in his movements, almost frenzied. I felt pleasure radiate from my core down my legs and up, up, through my breasts and heart until it exploded from me in a scream, and I trembled beneath him with the aftershock.

Greedily, I reached for him again, but he held my hand back with a smile. "Do not yet try to imitate perfection," he said. "We have the rest of our lives."

Chapter Six

WE MADE LOVE again that night and again the next morning when we awoke. I slept over, of course, lying with him in his upstairs bedroom on a king-sized bed with a dozen pillows. How many other women had slept here? I wondered, but the idea did not really upset me. He was welcome to his past. I had mine. It was the future that was ours together.

He made me breakfast—eggs and sausage, fresh orange juice and coffee, and served it to me while I was still in bed. Then we showered together, exploring each other's body with soapy hands, giggling like children playing "doctor." We made love one more time, unwrapping ourselves from bath towels made of soft cotton, letting the pleasure build slowly until release was essential.

He gave me a robe to wear around the house. It smelled of his cologne and I hoped it would stay with me when I was next alone.

At last I put on my dress, and we went for a walk around his property. Indeed, the backyard was well tended, festooned with flowers and two or three giant palms which, I thought with a smile, were appropriate for such a virile man.

Then we went back to the living room, where we ate sandwiches and watched a movie on television. In the middle of the afternoon, he suddenly stood up. "I'll take you home."

Home! I longed to say, I want this to be my home, but knew it was too early, that I could not, and I felt a sudden spasm of fear.

"So early?"

"Yes. I've got to catch a plane."

My heart lurched. "Where are you going?"

"To Cuba. I have an appointment with Castro's foreign minister."

"How long will you be gone?"

"A week, maybe. No more than ten days."

And will you return to me? I asked myself, not daring to voice the words.

"I'll call you when I get back."

I reached out to take his hand. "I'll wait for you."

"I'd like that."

He smiled at me, but again I felt afraid. Cuba. It seemed as far away as the moon. Were there women there who also loved him? When he came back, would he really call? I felt an urgent need to talk to Taylor, to get her counsel. What were white men like? I needed him—he had made me need him—and already he was leaving for a place I associated with danger.

"Wham, bam, thank-you-ma'am," I said angrily.

"Hey. That's not fair. And not true. I'm coming back."

"Promise?" I asked, ashamed of myself for begging.

"Absolutely. The deal's on my part, too."

"Then it's more than sex?"

"Much more."

Relieved, exhilarated, I laughed. "After last night and this morning, I'm sorry to hear it."

I wound up not telling Taylor much. Only that I had made love with Jeremy, that it was wonderful, and that I didn't know or much care what the future held—a lie. I asked her no questions, not wanting any disturbing answers, and went to bed soon after dinner.

I woke the next morning to reality. A familiar bed, no one by my side, a need for coffee, a workday ahead of me, clouds overhead. It was a struggle to get up, to put on clothes, to drive to the bank. But I did it, only barely aware of a void in my heart and a pleasant memory in my bones that told me the weekend really happened.

Almost as soon as I got to my desk, the phone rang.

"Jasmine, it's me," Greg said. "Have you made up your mind?"

"Almost."

"Well, please do. I can't talk long 'cause Patty's in the tub and could come out any second."

Not a word asking how I was; he thought only about himself. Sometimes, he made me sick.

"I'll need to know some answers," I said.

"What?"

"Like, have you even started to look for a job?"

"Sure. I go to the unemployment office. They have jobs posted there."

"And after that?"

"Go to the pool hall. I can always make spending money playing pool."

It was too much for me to handle. Here he was, with a college degree, he couldn't keep a job because of his hormones, and all he was doing was shooting pool!

"Haven't you applied at other engineering companies? I can't believe you can't get a job in your field."

"I don't want to go back to engineering. It's all run by whites."

"What does that mean?"

"That I'll be treated unfairly again, no matter what I do. In the old job, I was only used as an example. There was this white guy that was caught with his pants down, and they didn't fire him."

"With his boss, the vice president?"

"What difference does that make? They only fired me 'cause I'm black. If I was white, I'd still be working there."

He sounded stupid, making excuses like that, and I didn't want to hear more of it.

"Stop blaming people," I said. "It's your own fault, Greg, and you know it. Being black doesn't have anything to do with it." I was getting angrier and angrier.

He rattled on. "I guess that's what happens when you're the only black in a white company. I tell you, Jasmine, I'll never work at a white company again."

And so you'll throw away your education, everything our parents struggled to give to you, I thought. "What's happened to you?" I asked. "You never talked like this before. Your best friend at college was white. You didn't seem to have any trouble screwing a white woman at the company."

"I just got sick and tired of never getting anywhere because I'm black, that's what happened." There was so much anger in his voice I didn't even recognize the man I was talking to as my brother. He was never like this before. Now, his hatred oozed out of him like oil.

"As a matter of fact, I'm thinking of going to court," he said.

"Are you crazy? Do you want your affair to be made public? What do you think Patty would do if she found out?"

"What do you care about Patty's feelings? You never liked her anyway. No one in the family does."

"That may be true, but she deserves better than what you're about to do to her."

He sighed. "Jasmine, I didn't call to talk about my problems with Patty. I want to know if you'll co-sign for that loan or not."

I had decided to follow Jeremy's advice. Now, furious, I changed my mind.

"I don't think I can help you, Greg. It's too much of a chance. If you were really trying to help

73

yourself, that would be another matter. Have you asked Mom and Dad?"

"You know they can't afford to help. I really can't believe you won't help me out."

"I really can't believe you'd ask me to take a risk like that," I retorted. "Call me when you've made a real effort to get a job. When there's a chance you'll be able to pay the money back."

He slammed down the receiver.

My anger lasted all day and through dinner. Taylor was tactfully silent, and we ate without talking, then went to our rooms. I felt lonely and scared. Hollow.

The phone rang. If it's Greg, I thought, I'll hang up without saying a word.

The voice on the other end was muffled. Static came over the line. "Good news," the voice said.

"Jeremy!" It felt as though a light had switched on inside me.

"I actually got a line out. It isn't easy from here."

"Well—how are you?" I stuttered, suddenly unable to think of anything to say.

"Fine. I miss you."

"I miss you, too." Brilliant conversation!

"I can't talk long. What are you doing Saturday night?"

"I—I thought you weren't coming back for ten days."

"I got lucky. The foreign minister pushed up his interview. I'll be back Saturday afternoon. Want to come over to my place again? I'm hungry for you."

I was starved! "Oh, Jeremy, I can't. I promised my parents I'd come over. I haven't seen them in a long time, and they'd be so disappointed if I didn't show."

"That's fine. Why don't I come with you?"

"Would you really like to?"

"I'd love it." He hesitated. "You don't think they'd mind?"

"Mind? Why? They'll be happy I have a boyfriend."

"A *white* boyfriend."

I had actually forgotten he was white. To me he was only my boyfriend—my lover.

"They won't mind," I said. Really, though, I didn't know how they'd react. The subject had never come up.

"Anyway," he said, "they might as well know sooner as later. I plan to be around for some time."

Yes! My Sunday-night doubts vanished.

"Give me driving directions," he said, "and I'll meet you there. Only, make sure you get there before I do. I don't want the shock to be too great."

"Why not pick me up? It's only a little out of your way."

"Good idea. Then you can kiss me properly as a welcome home."

I'd kiss him, all right. Kiss him and much more!

I ran out of my room to tell Taylor about the call. She was sitting on the living room couch, head in her hands.

"What's the matter?" I put thoughts of Jeremy momentarily out of my mind.

"Cameron wants me to come over to talk."

"That's great!"

"I'm not sure. I don't know what he's going to say."

"He's going to want to get back together."

"I wish I believed that."

"What else could it be?"

"He's going to apologize. Tell me he's sorry. But in the end, he'll stay with them."

"Not if he loves you."

"*Because* he loves me. If we had just been screwing, nobody in his family would have cared. I'll bet Ben screwed hundreds of Japanese girls."

I gave her a hug. "You know what I think? I think you're depressed and afraid. But I have hope for you, Taylor. Cameron'll love you enough to fight for you."

"Would Jeremy fight for you?"

"Yes," I said. "I'm sure of it."

The rest of the week I put in some overtime. I wanted to be able at least to give Greg a little money, if not go so far as to co-sign a loan. Jeremy did not call again, but his silence did not disturb me. Saturday marched toward me like the sun around the earth.

On Saturday afternoon, I did some grocery shopping for my parents. I told them I was bringing a man with me, but did not warn them that he was white. I wanted to see their honest reactions, and did not want them to have time to prepare.

Jeremy arrived right on time. The kiss I gave him was great, but not all I said it would be. I was anxious about the coming meeting, and I think he was a little nervous, too.

In the car, I told him about Greg. He thought I had done the right thing. "Why should you give Greg what he wants," he said, "if he's not willing to work for it?" He drove with one hand, holding mine with the other. I felt secure.

When we got to my parents' house, my mother came outside. She looked at Jeremy, blinked, smiled, and hugged us both. She did not seem in the least upset. "Jasmine says you've become good friends," she told him. "I'm glad."

She led us into the house. "You're father's on the patio," she said. "I'll just go tell him you're here."

"No," I said. "We'll go with you." It was obvious that she wanted to warn him, and I wanted to stick to my plan.

"Very well," she said, and we followed her outside.

"Raymond, Jasmine's here, and she brought her friend," my mother said.

He was sitting with his back turned to us. Now he swung around and saw Jeremy. He gasped, frowned, then slowly got up. I ran to hug him.

Jeremy came over, extending his hand and smiling. My father hesitated, then took his hand and shook it warmly. It's going to be all right, I thought. At least, I think it is.

We sat down on the patio and my mother brought out iced tea. "When's the last time you spoke to your brother?" she asked.

"Last Monday," I said. "Everything seems fine." I

did not want to worry her, nor to betray Greg if he didn't want them to know.

My parents asked Jeremy about his family, and the conversation flowed easily. I looked at my beloved parents and my beloved man, and I was glad it all seemed to be going so smoothly. White or black, these people meant more to me than anyone else in the world.

My mother got up and went to the kitchen. I told her I'd help her. We made sandwiches.

"He's very nice, Jasmine," my mother said.

"Do you really think so?"

"You know me. I'd never have said it if I didn't believe it."

"It doesn't bother you that he's white?"

"Sure it does. A little. But he's your man. And if you don't care, why should I?"

"What about Dad?"

"I don't know. He was troubled at first, that's for sure. But then he seemed to relax. We'll talk about it, of course, after you've gone."

We carried the sandwiches to the dining room table. "Have you met his family yet?"

"No, not yet. Soon, though, I'm sure. Jeremy doesn't talk about them too much."

"Do you think they know you're black?"

"I doubt it."

"Do you think they'd like it?"

"To tell you the truth, Mom, I don't know what to think. Everything's happening so fast I haven't had time to worry about it."

Jeremy and my father were in a deep conversation about sports when we called them in to eat. The sandwiches were delicious, and I smiled as I watched Jeremy help himself to seconds. My mother and I cleaned up, and then we said good-bye. I admit I was thinking about making love with Jeremy and was anxious to leave, but Jeremy was relaxed and talkative, seemingly in no hurry. My parents invited us back, and we made a date for two weeks later. They walked us to Jeremy's car, and when we got there my mother hugged him as well as me, and my father warmly shook his hand.

"We like him," my mother whispered. I smiled with joy.

In the car, Jeremy smiled, too. "I really like your mom and dad. No wonder you're so special. You must have had a happy childhood with them."

"I did. And they liked you."

"I could sense it," he said. "They didn't seem to care that I was white."

"They were surprised at first, but they got used to the idea. It turned out you were a human being."

"I'm glad it went so well. It's one hurdle we don't have to worry about."

"What about meeting your parents?" I asked.

"I'll arrange it," he promised. "Soon."

We drove in silence for a while. My thoughts turned once again to love.

But Jeremy dashed them. "Do you mind if I take you home?" he said. "It's been a brutal day, what with the plane trip and the stress of meeting your parents. I want to make love to you, it's really all I thought about in Cuba, but I want to make love when I'm not this tired."

I looked at him closely. His face was drawn with fatigue and his eyes were red.

"Sick of me already?" I joked.

"You'll find out tomorrow. I'll pick you up at noon."

"It's a deal," I said, and put my hand high up on his leg.

The car swerved. "Hey," he said. "You'll kill us."

I kissed him on the cheek. "What a way to die."

We kissed passionately at my apartment door. The taste of his lips was still new to me, the smell of his cologne still intoxicating, and I thought for a moment of asking him upstairs, but I knew he was right. Tomorrow we would revel in each other; we had all the time in the world.

Taylor came in soon after I did. I could tell immediately that her evening had been awful. There were tear lines on her face, and her hands were trembling.

"He said good-bye?" I asked.

"Yes, only not because I'm black. It's worse than that."

We both sat down on my bed. "Worse?"

She started to cry. "He said he met someone else and that he didn't want to see me anymore."

I didn't know what to do, what to say. I just held her until she could cry no longer.

"Taylor," I said, "do you think he's telling the truth?"

"I don't know."

"When would he have had time to meet someone? You were always together."

"He could have met someone, all the same."

"Personally, I think he's running scared, that he's using the girlfriend line as an excuse. There can't be anybody else. He's just ashamed of himself, of being afraid of his brother."

She brightened. "You really think so? You aren't just saying that to make me feel better?"

"I'm not making it up. I see how you two look at each other. He loves you, Taylor. I'm sure. Even his parents tolerated you. But now his brother comes home, and suddenly there's another *woman* in the picture? It doesn't add up."

"Maybe you're right." She looked at me, managing a smile. "But what should I do? Do you think I should call him, make him tell me the truth?"

I handed her a Kleenex from the nightstand. "I think you should let him have some space. That's all he needs. When he's had a chance to think it through, he'll come around. I'm positive."

"How about you?" she said. "How are you and Jeremy doing."

"He met my parents tonight."

She was surprised. "No kidding! So soon? How did it go?"

"They liked him." I felt a little guilty because it had gone so easily.

"I'm glad for you, Jasmine. Really, I am."

But her eyes grew teary again, and I decided to

say no more. Besides, I hadn't met Jeremy's parents yet. There was no way of knowing how that would turn out.

Chapter Seven

THE ALARM WENT off, and I jumped up. I heard Taylor bustling around in her room getting dressed, too. We went to church together and sat up front. This time, I admit, I concentrated so hard on *not* thinking about Jeremy that I barely heard the sermon.

Still, Taylor and I chatted with the pastor before we left. Jeremy had promised to pick me up at noon, so I had plenty of time to get ready.

Back home, I took a long, hot bubble bath, then dried off and put my robe on. I stood in front of the mirror and started to part my hair, putting some curls on the top. Then I opened my robe, hoping to see myself through Jeremy's eyes. It was impossible. I knew I had good breasts and a thin waist, and that men found me attractive, but I was aware of my flaws. It was the body I had lived with all my life, and it didn't seem to be anything special to me. It was Jeremy I wanted to see naked, I reasoned, and when he looked at himself, he probably didn't think he was so remarkable, either. But he was. He was!

I didn't want to put on my makeup until I knew what I was going to wear. I looked in my closet and decided on a trapeze dress, brilliantly white, and I hunted around the bottom of the closet until I found the white slingbacks that went with it, and a small white purse. I laid everything out on the bed, then went back to the bathroom to do my makeup.

I didn't even bother with foundation; I just put some powder on my face and brushed my eyelids with rose blush. I wanted to create a casual look; he should not think I wore a lot of makeup. I put on some rose-colored lipstick, then added a little lip liner to darken it. I brushed some mascara on my lashes, spritzed my curls, and fingered each curl to perfection. The only thing missing was my pair of small sterling silver hoop earrings. It took me awhile to find them in my jewelry box. One day I'll organize my room, I thought. I sprayed perfume on my shoulders since they were bare, behind my knees, between my breasts, and inside my wrists. I walked back to my room, and put my dress on.

I looked at myself again in the mirror. The dress had spaghetti straps and a slim waist, and I decided against wearing a bra. The skirt flared a little and it was short, too. Maybe I shouldn't wear panties either, I thought, but no, that would be too forward, and Jeremy wouldn't like it. I loved my outfit, and did a little pirouette before the mirror. He knocked on the door. When I opened it, he stopped whatever he was about to say, and simply stood staring at me. Finally he spoke. "Wow," was all he could mutter.

We walked to his car. "I had thought we'd walk on the beach," he said, "but it's going to rain."

He was right. I hadn't even thought about the weather, but now I looked out the car window and saw ominous clouds on the horizon.

"Where should we go?"

"My house?"

I was hoping he'd suggest it.

"I've got some food at home. We can make a salad."

"I'm not very hungry," I said. I was, but only for him.

"Let's stop and pick up a movie," he said. "For later."

He chose *Guess Who's Coming to Dinner*. "It's a training film," he explained. "What to do when your white child brings home a black."

"But it's about a white girl bringing home a black man," I said.

He laughed. "I know. But it's the best I could do."

The rain had started by the time we got to his house, and we could hear thunder in the distance. We dashed inside. "I'll make us a drink," he said, and disappeared into the kitchen.

I stood at his picture window and looked out at the storm. I could see lightning flashes nearby; soon the storm would be upon us.

Yet I felt safe here, protected. Jeremy had turned

on the lights, and the room had a warmth I had not really appreciated before. I looked at the couch and felt my heartbeat speed up.

"Here's your drink," he said, coming up behind me. "Tell me if it's too strong."

I jumped. "You scared me."

There was a sudden clap of thunder, almost directly overhead. "I didn't think it would rain," he said. "They always say it will, but it never does."

The lights went out.

"Good," he said. "It saves me the trouble."

He led me over to the couch, his mouth on mine before I could speak. He had put the untasted glasses on the coffee table, his lips never leaving me. My heart pounded with anticipation. A flash of lightning lit up the room, and I could see his eyes, wild with desire. He kissed my eyes and ears, the tip of my nose, and again my mouth, sliding his tongue deep inside it, then keeping it still, letting me play with it to my own satisfaction. My knees were weak. We sat down on the couch, and he started to slide the straps of my dress down over my shoulders. I sat trembling as he slowly undressed me. He kissed me on the shoulders where the straps had been, then pulled the top of the dress down and exposed my breasts. My nipples were hard and erect. He kissed each nipple and continued down to my stomach.

"Let me help," I whispered, and I stood briefly to remove the dress and my panties, then I lay down on the couch, and moved his head back to my stomach. He had taken off his clothes and was kneeling by my side on the couch, and his head continued its downward exploration.

I gave a little moan and swung my legs over his shoulders, opening myself to his kiss with utter abandonment. It was all I wanted, his kiss on the center of my being. And when it came I screamed with pleasure and held his head in the vise of my legs so he could not move, only continue with what he was doing, taking me with him to ecstasy.

A clap of thunder, a bolt of lightning, only I wasn't sure whether they came from inside my head or from the elements outside. My body spasmed; I lost control of it.

In an instant, he was on top of me, entering me, telling me of his joy and pleasure. Waves of delight built up again inside me and I could feel his own passion increase. "Now," he shouted. "Now!" And his own scream was as loud as mine.

Suddenly we were laughing, and he rolled off the couch, falling so I would be on top of him, holding me to him with a gentle strength that forbade me to break away. I will stay like this forever, if that's what you want, I thought, and closed my eyes and kissed his neck and his chest, feeling my nipples once again harden against his chest.

Soon we were making love again, slowly, lingeringly, in peace as much as passion. Outside, the thunder receded and only a few streaks of lightning lit the sky. Now I sat up, put his head in my wet lap, and stroked his hair.

"You know," I said. "Black men are supposed to

be the best lovers. But I wouldn't trade you for anyone in the world."

Jeremy took me home early. He was still tired from his trip, and he had to get up early the next morning to write his article. I was tired myself, my body throbbing with a pleasant ache. The best kind of exercise, I thought with a smile.

I slept for ten hours and woke up feeling excited, as though this routine Monday held additional pleasures in store.

When I got to the office, I called Greg. Patty answered, and I asked to speak to him. I felt sorry for her, so I tried to be cordial. I still couldn't believe that she didn't know what was going on. If Jeremy had another lover, I thought, I'd sense it in a second.

Greg picked up the phone, keeping his voice muffled. I guessed that Patty was nearby.

"What have you decided?" he asked.

I fought down anger. He didn't even ask me how I was doing!

"I can't co-sign a loan for you. If I do and you can't pay it back, I'll be fired. But I can give you some money to help you out."

"Who've you been talking to? Did you tell Mom and Dad that I called you?"

"I haven't told anyone anything. What's the matter with you? Don't you think I can do something nice for you without asking someone's advice?"

"How much?" he said gruffly, without responding to my question.

"Fifteen hundred dollars. It's all I can afford right

now," I added, hating having to explain myself to him.

"You can't give me more?"

"I told you: It's all I can afford. Do you want the money or not?" I couldn't believe this was the same brother I had idolized when we were growing up.

"It's better than nothing," he said. "When will you be able to give it to me?"

"What if I come by tomorrow night?"

"I don't want Patty to know what's going on. Maybe I can come to your place."

"Sure."

"Give me the address."

He had never been to my apartment, I realized. My own brother! I told him the directions and we set a time. "But call before you come," I told him. If Jeremy wanted to see me, I wasn't going to let Greg interfere with that.

Jeremy did call, but only to talk. His work wasn't going well. "All I can do is think about making love with you," he said with a laugh. "So let's meet Friday night. We can go out to dinner, then back to my place. We can spend the weekend together."

Danielle and Simone had invited me to the beach on Saturday. I thought of asking Jeremy to go along, then decided against it. I didn't want him to see Danielle's disapproval. No, I'd just break the date with them, I thought.

"Fine," I told Jeremy. "Make it early Friday. I want you." I was astonished at my own brazenness.

"Not as much as I want you," he said, and then hung up.

That night, I couldn't sleep. My conversation with Greg had disturbed me deeply, and I wondered what had made him change so. Or was it I who had changed? Maybe he was always that way, only I hadn't realized it.

The next day, at lunch hour, I withdrew fifteen hundred dollars from my account. And when Greg called, I told him it was fine to meet me at eight. By working overtime, I would be able to repay myself, so I wasn't too concerned about that. What did trouble me was that I realized I didn't think Greg would ever repay me.

At home, I took a shower and put on shorts and a T-shirt. Greg didn't show until after nine; needless to say, I was furious.

"Do you know what time it is?" I asked him as soon as he arrived. "I left early because I thought you were going to get here at eight o'clock. I could have worked overtime to pay myself, because Lord knows I don't think I'm going to see any money from you."

He looked terrible. His face was unshaven, and there were deep rings under his eyes. "Please, Jasmine," he said. "Don't start on me. I get enough of that at home."

Yes. I was being mean. "I'm sorry."

"Will you fix me a drink?"

I could smell liquor on his breath, but I didn't say anything. I got him a glass of soda water. He looked at me as if I was crazy when I handed it to him.

"Nothing stronger for your brother?"

"This isn't a bar. Let me give you the money, then

if you want to spend it on drinks, that's your funeral."

His hard manner disappeared, and he sat at the dining room table and put his head on his arms on top of it. "I'm sorry, Jasmine. It's just that I've been so down lately, what with losing my job. I've been so *angry*. I know the reason they fired me was to make a point. I'm black; they wanted to show they could screw me any time they wanted. I swear, I'll never work for or even talk to a white man unless I absolutely have to."

I couldn't believe what was coming out of his mouth. I stood looking at him, wanting to cry. "You can find another job," I said, knowing it was fruitless to argue with him. "But you've got to try. White or black or whatever in between."

"Try? Don't you think I've *been* trying? I get up in the morning as if I'm going to work, and I pound the pavement looking for work."

"Stopping in occasionally for a drink and a game of pool."

"Only when I've used up my leads for the day."

"Why don't you tell Patty?" I urged. "Don't tell her about the other woman, but make up some excuse for having lost your job. Then she'll be able to help."

"Patty hasn't worked for years. She's used to not working, and she likes it. I was the provider, and that's what she expects of me. There's no way I'll be able to tell her to get a job."

He was a fool for hiding the situation from her, I thought. If a man's in trouble, he's got to tell his wife. But I didn't say anything. I just walked over to my purse and pulled out the envelope containing the money.

"Thanks," he said, getting up from the table and kissing me on the cheek. "I'll try to pay you back before Thanksgiving." Thanksgiving was only two months away. I didn't bother to ask him how he was going to do it.

"Patty and I plan to go over to the folks for Thanksgiving," he said, standing at the door.

"I'll be there with Jeremy," I said.

"Oho! Jeremy. Then there's a man in your life."

I remembered I had told him nothing about Jeremy. Now, I regretted saying anything at all. "He's a writer, an expert on Cuba. Mom and Dad have actually met him and like him a lot."

"You know I have to approve first," he said, smiling with some of his old charm.

"You'll meet him at Thanksgiving."

"Knowing about him, I'll be sure to come."

But you don't know that he's white, I thought. Given your present attitude, what will your reaction be?

The rest of the week passed in a blur. I put in as much overtime as I could, cancelled my date with Danielle and Simone, and spoke to Jeremy as often as possible, sometimes talking for as long as an hour.

On Thursday, he told me that plans had slightly changed. He would still pick me up Friday night, but on Saturday he had made a date with his parents so he could introduce me.

I had mixed feelings. I was thrilled that he liked

me enough to want to show me off to his folks, but I remembered Taylor's experience (Cameron had not called her since their breakup), and my heart filled with fear. Even people who say they're not biased, I thought, reveal bias when a stranger invades their family.

I got my hair done during lunch hour on Friday, and wished I'd had a chance to look for a new dress. Maybe Taylor would lend me one of hers. She dressed more conservatively than I normally did, and I wanted to appear as prim and proper as possible for Jeremy's parents.

I left right on time on Friday, went home, and quickly packed. When Taylor got back, I borrowed a dress from her, blue, high-necked—the dress, I'm sure, she wore when she met Cameron's family for the first time—then I asked her if she'd mind a little "girl talk."

"I'd love it," she said. "There's not much excitement now that Cameron's gone."

"It's him I want to talk about," I said. "Things are getting pretty serious with Jeremy. He's coming to pick me up tonight, for example, and I'm going to meet his parents tomorrow. What should I do? How should I act?"

She smiled and hugged me. "Act like Jasmine Smith," she said. "My wonderful friend who any man in the world would be lucky to get. I think I made a mistake with Cameron's family. I acted the way I *thought* they'd want me to act, and so they never really got to know me. I'm not sure if they did they'd have acted any differently, but I'd have felt

95

better about myself, and I'd have given myself a better chance. If their son could fall in love with the real Taylor, maybe they could have, too."

It was good advice, and I was determined to follow it. I'm me, I thought. A black woman with needs and desires and a family. A human being. If they don't like that, well—Jeremy does!

"All the same," I said, laughing, "can I borrow that dress?"

I packed it with my other things and was ready when Jeremy arrived. He sat and talked to Taylor for a while, and I could tell she liked him. I knew that of all my friends Taylor would be the most supportive of him, and he obviously felt easy with her.

I watched them talking and laughing together and felt a kind of happiness I had never experienced. If only this could go on forever, I thought. I have love and friendship, and my lover and my friend like each other. Maybe it's possible, barely possible, that it won't change.

But I had already had enough experience in life to know that it's never perfect. Be content in the moment, I warned myself. It won't last.

Our lovemaking that night was as good as ever. Jeremy seemed limitlessly inventive, finding places on my body to kiss and fondle to give me maximum pleasure, teaching me what pleased him most so he would never grow tired of wanting me.

We slept in his big bed, and I got up before he did to take my shower. When he opened his eyes, I was fully dressed, and he inspected Taylor's dress with a grin.

"Wearing that, they'll never suspect what you're like in bed," he said. "Should I tell them?"

"Only if I can tell them about you," I answered, and he threw a pillow at me.

I watched him get out of bed. He was naked, and his skin seemed to gleam in the morning light. Reggie, my ex, in his way had been beautiful, with a wonderfully developed chest and the legs of a long-distance runner. Jeremy was also beautifully built, but he seemed more muscular in his upper body. Both men were beautiful, but Jeremy had a grace to him I found irresistible. Why compare? I thought. The more beautiful is the one you love.

He showered and dressed quickly, for it was a long drive to his parents' house, and Jeremy had promised we would be there by lunch. Jeremy's parents lived in the suburbs, and when we drove through the neighborhood, I could tell they were well-off.

"Nervous?" Jeremy asked.

"A little. It's very beautiful here. It all seems so grand."

"They're looking forward to meeting you. It's a shame my sisters won't be there, but they live far away. We really only get together for holidays."

"I'm glad they won't be there. It's difficult enough meeting your parents. Five of you would be overwhelming."

As we drove, the houses got more and more spacious. Each had a manicured lawn and a mailbox out front. Most were two or three stories; all had two-car garages. There were kids playing in the yards or riding bicycles on the sidewalks. I felt as if we were driving through Mister Rogers's neighborhood. Everything looked so quaint and perfect. But nothing prepared me for the grandness of Jeremy's parents' house.

It was set a mile or so back from the street we were driving on. Like Jeremy's, it had a circular driveway, but here the driveway was huge, for the house itself was very large, with French doors and windows everywhere. It looked like an English mansion, and I found myself hoping that its owners were simpler than the place where they lived.

Jeremy stopped in front of the entrance. He opened my door for me, and I stepped out, glad that I had borrowed Taylor's dress. The front door was open, so we walked into a marble foyer with a huge mirror on one side and a painting of a man in uniform on the other.

"My great-grandfather," Jeremy said, catching my look. "He fought in the Civil War."

For the South, I thought. So they could keep their slaves.

"For the wrong side," Jeremy said, as though reading my mind. "He died an alcoholic."

A little dog came out of nowhere, yapping and dancing around my ankles.

Jeremy picked him up. "This is Brandy," he said. "Brandy, meet Jazz."

I patted the dog and Jeremy handed him to me. "Hi, Brandy," I said, feeling slightly less uncomfortable.

"Jeremy, is that you?" I heard a sweet voice coming from the room to our right.

"Yes, Mom," he said, holding my hand and leading me toward her.

She was sitting in an armchair in the living room, and rose to greet us when we came in. The room itself was wood-paneled, full of immense furniture, with high ceilings and mammoth paintings which seemed to come from another age. I knew everything was supposed to be beautiful, but I felt it was all a little musty. Give me Jeremy's modern house any time, I thought.

Mrs. Collins was a tall woman, with snow white hair, blue eyes, and cheeks that seemed made of white china. She was dressed in a flowing dress, with a flower design, and I rather cruelly thought that she belonged with the furniture.

If she was surprised that I was black, she showed no appearance of it. She hugged and kissed her son, then turned to me. "This must be Jasmine," she said.

Of course! Jeremy must have warned her that I was black. I had the sense that she was giving a performance.

"I'm Jeremy's mother," she said, taking my hand. "Please call me Felicia. Everyone does."

Her smile was cordial and her eyes were kind. I began to change my first impression.

"Where's Dad?" Jeremy asked.

"He went to the store for some wine. We thought we'd have some with lunch. But would you like a drink now?" she asked me.

I looked at Jeremy. He shrugged. "Maybe a glass of sherry," I said.

"Gin and tonic for me," Jeremy said. His mother poured from bottles on a sideboard and handed us our drinks.

"Well, well, this must be Jasmine," a voice boomed behind us.

"Pop," Jeremy said, walking to his father and giving him a hug. He came over to me and shook my hand.

"I've heard a lot about you," he said. "You seem to have quite captured my son."

"I hope everything you've heard is good," I said with a nervous laugh.

"Almost too good," he said. "That's why we wanted to see for ourselves."

There was nothing confrontational in his manner, but his words made me uneasy. "Just be Jasmine Smith" echoed in my head. And remember: Jeremy's here and he's on your side.

Nevertheless, I was pretty quiet for the next few minutes while Jeremy and his parents talked about people and events that meant nothing to me. Soon, we went in to lunch, in the equally musty dining room on the other side of the foyer. There were china plates set on a linen tablecloth, silver knives, forks, and spoons, wineglasses empty and water glasses already full. Mrs. Collins went to the kitchen, reappeared carrying soup for all of us, then poured us white wine from a bottle already opened on a sideboard.

I tasted the soup. It was cold, made of potatoes and cream, and I thought it was delicious, as were the chicken salad that followed it and the sponge cake with fresh berries, our dessert.

Jeremy's parents were unfailingly nice to me, asking me questions about my family, my job, my friends, my childhood. They drew me out, and I enjoyed talking about myself, particularly because I could sense Jeremy's approval. I was really only unhappy when we were being served. Then I felt uncomfortable. How different our lives were! Jeremy from this wealth; I from a modest home. One more factor to keep us apart.

We left soon after lunch, after I had helped Mrs. Collins do the dishes. Jeremy claimed that we had to meet friends, but I knew that it was because he could sense I was under some strain and wanted to make things easy for me.

Our parting was warm, cordial. Mrs. Collins hugged me and asked us back again. Mr. Collins shook my hand and told me that I was beautiful and that Jeremy was a lucky man.

When we got in the car, though, I burst into tears.

"What's the matter?" Jeremy asked, concern in his eyes and voice.

"It was the house," I said. "It's too grand. Oh, your parents were as nice as they could be, and they did everything right, but I still felt *black*, different, not one of them. And they're so rich!"

Jeremy thought for a moment. "What if it had been a black family's house?"

"I wouldn't have felt so uncomfortable."

"So it was their whiteness, not their wealth, that got to you?"

"I suppose so."

"Well, the difference in color doesn't matter, Jazz, really it doesn't. My parents looked at you as though you were one of us, a woman, the woman I love."

"How do you know?" I sobbed.

"For one thing, my mother asked you to call her by her first name. She only does that with friends."

"She asked me before I had said a word."

"Yes, she wanted to be friends from the start. And my father adored you."

"How do you know?"

"From the way he looked at you. He wasn't kidding when he said he thought you were beautiful. In fact, I think he's a little jealous of me."

I had stopped crying. Now I leaned over and kissed him.

"What was that for?"

"For being you," I said. "For making it easy for me. For knowing what I'm scared of and doing something about it."

He said nothing, just kept his eyes on the road. I wanted to tell him that I loved him, but I held back. I wasn't sure I did. Maybe it was only the sex, the newness of it, the very fact that he was white and I black, the excitement of that, like discovering an unknown country. I had never said those words to any man, not even Reggie, and I knew I would not say them until I was sure, until no doubt existed.

"Oh, Jazz," he said, and squeezed my hand as though he wanted to make love to it.

But he did not say "I love you" either.

Chapter Eight

WHEN JEREMY OPENED the door to his house, the phone was ringing.

"Don't answer it," I said. "I want to make love."

He laughed. "It may be important."

There was a phone in the foyer, and he answered it there. "It's for you," he said, holding the receiver out to me. "Your father."

"What is it?" I said into the phone, suddenly scared. He would never have called me at Jeremy's—I hadn't even given him the number—unless it was something urgent.

"Your mother fell down the stairs. She's banged up pretty bad."

My heart was pounding. "Where are you?"

"At the hospital. She broke her leg, and they had to fix it. Your mother got up early this morning to get a glass of water. I told her to put on the light, but before I got the words out of my mouth, she had fallen. I found her at the bottom of the stairs and called the doctor."

"And what does he say now?"

"That she'll be fine. That is, that she'll live. He doesn't know how well she'll be able to walk."

Jeremy brought me a chair and I sat on it. A broken leg is serious for someone sixty-five years old. I knew that it would take a long time to heal and might not heal correctly.

"I'll be there as soon as I can."

"There's really no need," my father said. "She's pretty doped up, might not even recognize you. Besides, you're with Jeremy. I don't want to spoil that."

"Nothing can stop me," I said. "Who's going to look after *you*?"

I hung up and told Jeremy what had happened. He started for the door. "I'm going with you."

"Oh, Jeremy, would you?"

"What was it you said to your father? 'Nothing can stop me'? 'Who's going to look after *you*?' "

I kissed him. "Just let me tell Greg."

I called my brother. He seemed deeply distressed about the accident. "Do you think she can talk on the phone?" he asked. "I want to call her."

"Call her? You should go to see her."

"I can't," he said. "Patty wants me to do some things around the house. I can't put them off."

"Not even when your mother's in the hospital?"

"She not dying," he said coldly.

"I can't believe you! I never thought I'd say this to you, Greg, but I'm disappointed in you. Keep the damn money, I don't want it back, but don't call me again."

I slammed down the phone. Jeremy was looking at me, and I ran into his arms.

"He's changed so," I said. "It's Patty. She's made him her servant."

"Then he's Patty's problem, not yours. I can understand your unhappiness, but you've got to realize he's a grown man and not your responsibility."

"I don't love him anymore," I sobbed.

He hugged me tighter. "Once you get over your anger, you will."

He led me to the car. "Do you know how to get there?"

I dried my tears. "I think so." We started off. "Thanks for being here," I said. "I'm really worried. She isn't very strong, and I'm afraid she won't be able to get around like she used to."

"It may not be as bad as you think. Let's wait and see."

He drove carefully, with enormous concentration. I knew he was tired from all the driving he had already done that day, but he said nothing about it.

At last, we pulled into the hospital parking lot. He took my hand. "It's going to be all right. I promise."

The attendant at the desk gave us my mother's room number, and we entered the elevator. When we got off, I saw my father sitting in a chair in the hallway.

"How's Mom?" I asked, alarmed. Why was he sitting outside if she was in the room?

"She's in a lot of pain. The doctor's with her now,

and he's given her another painkiller. She should feel better soon. Only I don't like it that she's had to take so many drugs."

"A few days' worth won't hurt her," Jeremy said. "For now, the main thing is to make her comfortable."

My father looked at him and smiled. "It was good of you to come," he said. "I liked you the first time I met you, but I wasn't sure about you. Now I see you're a fine man."

"I'm Jazz's friend," Jeremy said. "Her mother's in trouble, which means that she's in trouble. Of course I came with her."

"Not everyone would."

"Do you need me to get any of Mom's things from the house?" I asked. "A bathrobe? Some slippers?"

I felt sorry for my father. He looked worn out, and I knew he would have to be alone in the house for the next few days.

Dad gave me a list of things, and Jeremy drove me to get them so we could be back by the time my mother was ready for visitors.

It took no more than ten minutes for me to pack a small bag for her, and we drove back immediately. "I really don't know how to thank you," I told Jeremy in the car.

"You can start by not thanking me at all. I *want* to be here for you—and for your family. I guess you don't realize how much I want to be part of your life, and how much I want you to be part of mine."

He pulled the car into a rest area on the side of the road. "Why are we stopping?" I asked.

"Because I have something important to say, too

important to say when I'm driving." He turned to face me and took both my hands in his. "I said you've become a very important part of my life. I know we've only known each other a little while. I know there'll be all sorts of trouble ahead because I'm white and you're not. I know that our backgrounds are completely different, and that some of our friends won't like one another. But each time I see you, I'm more and more sure that I want to share myself with you, share things with you, *be* with you." He looked at me, and his intensity made me a little frightened. "What I'm saying is, I'm falling in love with you—for the first time in my life, I'm falling in love."

I gave a cry of joy. "Oh, Jeremy!"

"And what I want to know," he went on, "what I *have* to know, is whether you think you could ever love me back."

Love him back! I loved him already, loved his kindness, his sense of humor, his body, his mind. And yet I hesitated in my answer. This was, I knew, a turning point in my life, a giving up of everything I had known for a man I barely knew, for a life that could not be predicted.

I measured my words, careful to be clear. "Yes, I could love you back. There's no question of it."

He moved to kiss me but I avoided his touch. "Hear the rest of it."

He settled back behind the wheel, looking straight ahead. "Everything's happened so fast," I said. "Knowing you, making love with you, being with you—all that's had me so excited I haven't been able to think about the future. I want to be with you now and tomorrow. But I don't want to think beyond that; it's all too new. You're ready to make a commitment; I'm not. We're too different, not only in skin color, but in background. Yes, I remember what you said to me on the beach, and what my own heart said, too, and I did not make love with you lightly. But I need a little more time and a little more thought. Can't we go on as we have before, loving each other daily, looking forward to the next date, the next time we make love? Let's do that and leave it at that, at least for the moment."

While I talked, visions of Taylor and Danielle flashed through my head. It felt as if my brain were being torn apart. I started to cry.

"Hey," Jeremy said. "It's enough for me that you said you might love me. I'm not looking for quick answers. I know the problems. I just want to think that there's a chance."

This time it was I who moved to kiss him. He turned so that our lips touched, and he held me tight. He needs me, I thought. For whatever reason, he really needs me.

The thought made me smile. "There's a good chance," I said.

We did not stay long at the hospital. We were able to see my mother, but she was heavily sedated, so the conversation was brief. Dad didn't even come into the room with us.

"We're here." I said. "Jeremy and I."

She smiled weakly. "That's nice of him." I wanted to wrap her in a blanket and take her home with me. There were wires everywhere; I couldn't understand why, if the only thing wrong with her was a broken leg.

"Are you in pain?" Jeremy asked.

She laughed. "They have me so drugged up, baby, all I can feel is sleepy. Promise to come back and visit. Jasmine, take care of your father." Her eyes closed.

I promised I'd come back tomorrow, and kissed her with tears in my eyes. I didn't want her to be in pain and I didn't want my father to be alone. Jeremy gave her a kiss, also, and we walked into the hall.

"Daddy, why does she have all those wires in her?" I asked.

"She has a small heart murmur. The doctor says it's just a precaution." He smiled at us. "You two need to go home. There's nothing more you can do here. I'll be fine."

I knew that he was trying to be strong for me, but I knew, too, that I had to be strong for both of us. "All right, but I'll be back tomorrow. And I'll be home if anything happens. Call me even if it's the middle of the night."

"Home?" Jeremy asked as we left.

"Do you mind? I don't think I'd be much fun for you. I'm just too worried."

"You don't have to be 'fun.' I just want to make sure you're all right."

His presence would be too much pressure, I knew. I didn't want to have to think about us with my mother so sick. "No, really," I said. "It's better this way. I'll see you next weekend."

"Okay," he said, although I could tell he was disappointed. "I'll drive you home."

I tried to sleep in the car, but I was too restless. "I hope my father'll be all right," I said. "I didn't want to leave him there, but I knew he wouldn't go home, and there was nothing for me to do. I'll relieve him tomorrow."

"I'll come with you."

"You're a dear, but no thanks. It'd be boring for you, and you'd just be in the way."

"Your father's a wonderful man. I'm glad he was honest with me."

"I hope he'll be all right. I worry about him, Jeremy. What if something happened to my mother? It'd kill him."

"Your mother will be fine. Believe me, I've seen far worse accidents than hers and everything turned out all right."

I kissed him on the neck. "Okay, Dr. Jeremy. I'll stop worrying."

"Do you want to get something to eat?"

"No, thanks. I'm too upset. All I want to do is watch some television and go to sleep early."

He drove me to my door. "I'm sorry this has spoiled our weekend," I said.

He kissed me, then held me at arm's length and looked into my eyes. "Me, too. But we have thousands more weekends, and your parents need you. I understand."

"You're terrific," I said.

"Just spare some thought for what I've said." He grinned. "And go on trying to love me."

I opened the door. "You're the boss."

"Call me tomorrow to let me know how things are."

"Soon as I've seen her. I'll call from the hospital."

"Sleep well," he said.

I knew I wouldn't. I was nearly asleep when the phone rang.

"Jasmine, it's Greg. Did you see Mom? How's she doing?"

"Why didn't you see for yourself?" I asked in disgust.

"I'll be there tomorrow. Is she in any pain?"

He sounded like he really cared. I knew that he was scared, but I could only be here for him if he'd let me.

"I'm sorry I snapped at you earlier. I was just worried about Mom. She looks awful and they're monitoring a heart murmur, but I don't think she's in real trouble. Both the doctor and Dad say she'll be fine."

"Are you going tomorrow?" Greg asked.

"Sure. I'll go right after church."

"I'll meet you."

"In church?"

He laughed. "That's asking too much of me. At the hospital."

As soon as I hung up, the phone rang again.

"I called to wish you good night," Jeremy said.

His voice brought on a longing I could hardly

explain. "I wish I was with you," I said. "It was a mistake to let you go."

"No. You did the right thing."

There was a silence.

"What are you doing?" he asked.

I laughed. "Trying to love you."

"And—?"

In that instant, all the strain of the day—his parents, mine, Jeremy himself—came flooding over me.

"I need you," I wailed.

He grunted with pleasure. "Good. Keep it up."

Taylor came home, but I was too exhausted to get out of bed to talk to her. Instead, I prayed for my mother and father and Greg. Then I prayed for the strength to deal with my new relationship and the strength to be available for my family. After I finished praying, I felt at peace, and I drifted off into a sleep of resignation.

Chapter Nine

THE NEXT DAY, my mother was much better. She was in traction, and would remain in the hospital for another week. But those terrible wires were gone, and she was far less doped up than she had been the night before.

Greg came in a little after I did, shaved and wearing a sport jacket and tie. He winked at me when he entered and couldn't have been nicer to our mother, who beamed at his appearance and continued smiling through his jokes and comments. I was happy to see him, but soon realized that his behavior was an act; that underneath the smile was a deep sadness that he could not hide from me.

I knew what was wrong, of course, and did not press him about it. If he wanted to keep his firing from our parents, that was his privilege and I was certainly not about to break his trust.

When I arrived, my father went home to get some rest, so it was my mother who brought up the subject of Thanksgiving. "I'm sure I'll be recovered by then," she said, "so the party's on. Jasmine, you bring Jeremy, and I do hope, Greg, that you and Patty will come."

"It'll be too much work for you," I said. "Why not put it off till next year?"

"Nonsense. This year *and* next year. Every year."

"Then I'll come early to help out. I'll make the pies at home and bring them."

"They won't be as good if you make them," Greg said, laughing, but my mother was obviously pleased, and I vowed to let her do as little as possible.

"Please do come," I said to Greg as we were leaving. "It's been such a hard time for her, and I know she misses you."

"It's Patty," he replied. "She feels uncomfortable with them. She thinks they don't like her."

"But the way to change that is to give them a chance to know her. I'm sure we'd all like her more if she were more friendly."

"You're right, but she doesn't believe it."

"Please make her come."

"I'll try, but I can't promise."

"Do your best," I said.

"You know I will."

I drove to Jeremy's house, pleased that I could so easily find the way. He was at his desk in his study, but came down to kiss me when I rang the doorbell.

"Here," he said, handing me a small box.

"What is it?"

"A present."

"But it's not my birthday, or a holiday, or—"

"It doesn't have to be a special day for me to give

you a present. Aren't you going to open it?" He was smiling.

Inside the box was a silver key ring attached to a silver medal. On the medal was inscribed his name for me, Jazz, and on the ring itself a single key.

"What's the key for?" I asked.

"The front door."

"Here?"

"Yes. I want you to think of this as your house, as well as mine. If you want to move in permanently, fine. If you don't, then that's fine, too. Either way, I want you to be able to come and go when you please, even if I'm not here."

I felt overwhelmed. He looked at me with such longing and such love that I thought my heart would melt. I started to cry.

"What's the matter?" His eyes were troubled.

"I never thought I'd feel like this. When people said 'You'll know it's love when it feels like love,' I didn't understand what they were talking about. But now I do. Now I know what love feels like." I put my arms around him and kissed him hungrily, savoring the taste, the smell, the warmth. "It feels like you."

I did not move in with him. I needed a little more time, a little more space, to be sure, and besides, he lived much farther away from work than I did and I had no intention of quitting my job.

Still, I moved some clothes and toiletries into his house, and I spent the weekends with him, weekends full of talk and laughter, movies on the VCR, jazz on the CD player, and lovemaking. Lots of lovemaking.

I came to his house the night before Thanksgiving

and made the pecan and lemon meringue pies I had promised my mother. We left early the next morning, since I didn't want my mother, who was still on crutches, to walk around much even in her own home. Jeremy was delighted. "While you two work in the kitchen, I can get to know your father better," he said.

I felt comfortable with him, like a longtime lover, though each day with him brought something wonderful and new. He seemed to understand my feelings as much as I did—like saying he wanted to know my father better.

My parents met us with hugs and kisses. I loved spending the holidays with them; it made me remember when I was growing up. Walking into the kitchen, I could smell the turkey and candied yams cooking.

"Now you just sit down," I told my mother. "This is my show from now on. I do the work. Your job is to talk to me." I took down plates to begin setting the table.

"Are Greg and Patty coming?" I asked.

"Greg called and said they were. I hope so. You know it would make us both happy. He hasn't been to see me since he came to the hospital."

"He'll come," I said, but I wasn't sure.

At around two, we decided to wait for Greg and Patty no longer. The food was ready, and we didn't want to spoil it by overcooking or letting it get cold. I sat beside Jeremy, and my father led us in a prayer.

"We have a tradition here," I told Jeremy when

the prayer was over. "We all have to say why we're thankful, one by one. You start, Mom."

She was thankful for her restored health and for the love of her family, who stood by her. My father was thankful she had recovered, that we had enough to eat, and for his children, whom he loved.

"Now you," I said to Jeremy.

He stood up. "I'm not good at speeches," he said, "but I'm good at thanks. I'm thankful first of all for Jasmine, who means more to me than even she knows. And I'm thankful for this Thanksgiving, with a family as warm and loving as you. Finally, I'm thankful to be me, for I'm the one you've asked to share it with you."

He sat down, blushing. My parents applauded. It was my turn.

I started to speak, then stopped. My heart was too full. "Go on," my father said.

"I'm thankful for my mother and my father. I've always been thankful you are who you are, and I always will be. And this year, I'm thankful for Jeremy. He's been here for me when I needed him. He's been my best friend. Because of him, this has been the happiest year of my life."

We began to eat. There was a commotion in the front hall. My father and I sprang up. "They're here," my father said.

Greg and Patty had come after all! They were late, they brought no contribution to the dinner, not even flowers, but at least they showed up, and I was grateful for small favors. "Hi, Greg. I just about gave up on you." I kissed him. "Hi, Patty. We're just eating, but maybe you want a drink first."

She looked so sad and uncomfortable that I suddenly felt sorry for her. We hadn't been very nice to her, it's true. And no matter what she did to Greg, she was a human being and she meant no harm.

She was obviously nervous, but she smiled at us all, and dutifully gave Dad a hug. She's trying, I thought. Good for her.

They followed me and Dad into the dining room. "Hello, Mom," Greg said, and then he stopped short and his mouth dropped open. Patty saw what he saw, and she gave a little scream, then covered her mouth with her hand.

"Greg, Patty, this is Jeremy," I said. "Jeremy, my brother and sister-in-law."

Jeremy got up and extended his hand. Greg took it, but the look on his face was one of disgust, as though he were holding a dead animal. I looked at Jeremy to see if he had noticed anything, but his expression was bland. He shook hands with Patty, too, who smiled at him shyly and backed away as soon as she could.

We all sat down to eat. My father asked Greg how his job was going, and Greg said "fine," without giving any details. Patty didn't say anything about it. I figured Greg hadn't yet told her he'd been fired.

The tension in the room made us all uneasy, and we ate quickly, without much pleasure. Only Jeremy seemed to enjoy his food. He had seconds of everything and both kinds of pie.

After dinner, I cleared the table and Patty followed me to the kitchen.

"Is he your boyfriend?" she asked.

"Yes."

"You mean you've—"

"Made love to him? Many times. Is there anything wrong with that?"

"I don't have a problem with it," she said after a pause. "But I don't think your brother likes it one bit."

I could feel my anger rise. "Frankly, I don't care what he thinks. He has no say in my life. Besides, he has a lot more to worry about than who I'm dating."

Greg came in, obviously furious. He turned on me immediately. "I can't believe you brought a white boy into our parents' house," he said. "Have you no pride at all?"

"You're a fine one to talk about pride. You don't even have a job."

"What did you say?" Patty asked, staring at me.

"I said he didn't have a job. I had to loan him money, and he can't pay it back."

Patty wheeled on her husband. "Is this true?"

He looked as if he'd been punched. "Yes," he muttered.

I didn't want her to learn from me what had happened. "I'm sorry, Greg," I said. "But I was so mad at you about Jeremy, it just slipped out."

"What does she mean?" Patty asked her husband. "Why didn't you tell me?"

I could see they were in for a fight, so I left the kitchen and went to the living room. Jeremy and my father were talking quietly. Mom had fallen asleep in her chair.

"We'd better go," I said.

"So soon?" Dad looked troubled.

"Mom's tired, and I'm mad at Greg."

"Why?"

"Because he doesn't think Jeremy should be here."

"Yes," Jeremy said softly. "I thought that's what was going on."

"We'll come back next weekend," I told my father, and I kissed him good-bye. "Tell Mom I love her and I'll call her later," I said. "Come on, Jeremy."

He shook hands with my father and followed me obediently. In the car, I described everything that had happened.

"You shouldn't have told Patty," he said. "He has every right to be upset, his sister's going out with a white man. In time, let's hope he gets over the shock."

"I know," I said. "I feel terrible that I betrayed him."

"Is it that, or is it that he's angry I'm white?"

"Both," I admitted. "I had so wanted him to like you. To not care what color you are."

"We'll run into a lot of prejudice. This is just an example of it."

"Greg's my big brother. It hurts that it comes from him."

"Because now you have to choose between us?"

I nodded miserably.

"I can see that it's tough," he said. "If I had to

choose between my sisters and you, I'd feel the same way. But maybe we can grow to be friends in time. I'll sure do my best to make it happen."

"Why can't things be easy?" I wailed.

"Because we're all human beings," Jeremy said. "Complicated as can be."

He took me back to my apartment. I would spend the weekend at his house, but I had promised to be with Taylor on Thanksgiving evening. Her parents lived in California, and Taylor didn't have the money to visit them during both Thanksgiving and Christmas; she decided on Christmas. This was a particularly hard time for Taylor, I knew. It's lonely to be away from your family on a holiday, and it was particularly hard on her now that Cameron had gone.

I kissed Jeremy good-bye and went into the apartment. "Taylor!" I called. "You home?"

I heard rustling behind her closed door, then laughter. A man's laugh!

In a moment, the door opened, and Taylor came out, looking sheepish and wearing only a bathrobe. Standing behind her, dressed in slacks and a still-unbuttoned shirt, stood Cameron.

"Happy Thanksgiving, Jasmine," Taylor said. "We were just—"

I giggled. "I know what you were doing. But I thought—"

"I've come back to her," Cameron said. "I don't care what the problems are, I don't care what the future holds. I only know that I couldn't live without her—*could not live*."

"So here he is," Taylor grinned. "My man."

Looking at their happiness, I felt tears of joy come to my own eyes. I thought of how awful Greg had been to Jeremy, and how awful I had been to Greg, and that all of that, terrible as it was, didn't matter in the face of what I felt for Jeremy. "I'm so glad for you," I said, choking back a sob. "So really, really glad."

I decided to use my new key. Though they were cordial and polite to me, Taylor and Cameron obviously wanted to be left alone in the apartment, so I drove to Jeremy's house without telling him I was coming and let myself in as quietly as possible.

He was not in the living room, kitchen, or study, so I peeped into the bedroom, and found him fast asleep on his back in bed, naked, the covers thrown off and hiding only one leg. His hair was tousled, and in the innocence of sleep he seemed like a little boy, until I looked lower and saw that he was most definitely a man.

That part of him fascinated me, and I sat gently on the bed next to him and took it in my hand. He stirred but did not wake, and urged on by a sudden rush of desire, I bent down and took him in my mouth.

I heard him moan, and looked at his face. He was watching me with intense concentration, his lips open with pleasure, and when I stopped for a moment he put his hand on my head as a signal to go on. I increased pressure and speed, nearly as excited as he was. I had never done this before, not even with Reggie, and could not believe the pleasure it brought me to give so much joy to the man I loved.

I did not take my mouth away until after he had climaxed and I felt him go calm. He reached for me, wanting to take off my dress, but I gently took his hand away. "This night is for you," I said. "You alone. Because I love you."

He smiled and reached for me again. I undressed by myself and slipped into bed next to him, snuggling into his arms. Soon, though, I turned on my side, my back to him. He fitted himself against me, spoon fashion, his hands cupping my breasts, and in this position we both fell asleep.

I woke to the smell of coffee and frying bacon. In a few minutes, Jeremy came into the room, stark naked, bearing a tray with orange juice, eggs and bacon, toast, and coffee.

"Breakfast for my lady?" he asked.

"Can you not afford clothes?"

"My lady did not seem to mind last night."

I sat up, letting the sheet fall from my breasts. "Well, if you don't mind, I guess I won't."

He set the tray down on a nearby table, and came to sit next to me, his expression suddenly serious. Then he took my face in both hands, kissed me, kissed me again, then pushed my head away only far enough so he could look directly into my eyes.

"I love you, Jazz," he said. "Will you marry me?"

My heart became a joyous animal, leaping in my

chest. My doubts disappeared. I knew I would love this man forever.

"Yes," I cried. "Yes, I'll marry you! You've just made me the happiest person in the whole wide world!"

We kissed, and his hand touched my breast. Laughingly, I pushed it away, but he insisted, and soon I was responding, feeling him grow hard, wanting him.

"The breakfast," I gasped, pulling him on top of me.

His hands were all over me, his need urgent. "We have time to cook another."

Actually, all we had was orange juice and coffee. I was too excited to eat.

"We should look for an engagement ring," Jeremy said. "And set a date."

"January," I told him. "Everybody else gets married in June, but ours is so special it should be as far away from the others as possible."

"January it is, then. What about the ring? I'll meet you at lunch hour next week, and we'll buy it together."

"No," I decided. "You pick it out. Surprise me."

"Only if you pick out the wedding rings."

I solemnly shook his hand. "It's a deal."

I called my parents. My mother answered the phone.

"Jeremy and I are getting married," I shouted.

There was a long pause. Then, "Oh, honey, I'm so glad for you. When?"

"January."

"Do you want the ceremony here?"

"I haven't had a chance to think about it, or talk it over with Jeremy."

"When you decide, let me know."

She summoned my father to the phone. I told him the news. "I'm very, very happy of course," he said, "but I wish you were marrying a black man."

"I thought you liked Jeremy!"

"I do. Very much. It's not because of me that I said that, but because of you. You're going to face problems you can't even imagine. Your children will, too."

I knew he was right, and some of my giddiness disappeared. "It doesn't matter," I told him. "I love him too much to let any problems interfere."

He forced good cheer, but I could tell he was worried. "Of course. You're both strong, and you'll manage. All the same—"

Jeremy took the phone from me. "Mr. Smith? All I want to say is that I love your daughter and I'll do everything in my power to make her happy."

He listened for a while, laughed, and then hung up. "What did he say?" I asked.

"That you were too good for me, and that if I didn't make you the happiest woman alive, he'd break my knees."

"My dad's always had good judgment," I told him.

I called Taylor with the news. She was overjoyed. "That means we can face the world together," she said, and I knew having Taylor and Cameron as part of our lives would make the going easier.

Simone, too, was thrilled with my announcement. She promised to throw me a wedding shower. Danielle, though, was more cautious. "I'm happy for you," she said, "but you know how I feel about black women marrying white men. It can only mean trouble."

She's jealous, I thought, brushing off the fact that she and my father might be right as though it were a bothersome fly.

We made plans over the weekend. There would be a church service, then a reception at my folks' house. We would go to Cancun for our honeymoon. We would live at his house, even though it meant a long commute for me.

How I loved those talks. I had imagined them in my fantasies; now those fantasies were coming true.

On Sunday morning we drove to the beach. Jeremy bought me a new bathing suit as an engagement present; it showed off my figure in a way that made his eyes gleam. As we walked along the sand, letting the waves lap at our toes, I asked him if he had told his parents about the marriage.

"I discussed it with them even before I proposed."

I was astonished. "What did they say?"

"Frankly, they weren't happy. It's nothing personal against you; they just barely know you. They didn't like the idea of my marrying a black woman. Still, at the end of our talk, they told me that if I was happy, then they were happy too. I said that the more they knew you, the more they'd love you."

"What if they'd forbidden you to marry me?"

"I'd have married you anyway."

I should have asked, Then why did you consult with them before proposing to me? But I was scared of the answer. Married me anyway? I wasn't sure.

"Have you told Greg and Patty?" Jeremy asked.

"No."

"How come?"

"I just haven't gotten around to it."

"You mean you're frightened about his reaction."

"I suppose so."

"You've got to face it," he said. "You've got to face everything."

Chapter Ten

I WENT HOME Sunday night, but stayed up till almost two o'clock, talking things over with Taylor. In the morning I showered and dressed and got to work early, anxious to tell my coworkers the news.

"How goes it with you and the new beau?" Brigitte asked, almost as soon as I came in.

"As a matter of fact, we got engaged over the weekend. I was going to tell you later, but since you asked—"

The look on her face was hilarious. She couldn't believe what I had told her.

"You're kidding!" she said. "You can't be serious about marrying a white man. Haven't you taken this a little too far?"

"I haven't taken anything too far. Jeremy proposed and I said yes. It's you who are going too far. You don't even have a man, and you're trying to tell me how I should live my life. All you do is screw around, hoping someone will marry you, and now you're jealous because I found a man before you did."

My words left her speechless. She backed away from me and went back to work. I hadn't meant to be cruel to her, but she'd made me mad with her prejudice. I suppose I was being a little defensive. Anyway, when everyone was going off for lunch, I approached her to say that I was sorry.

"I didn't mean to go off on you like I did, but I was ticked off that you couldn't understand me marrying a white man. I really love him, and I didn't feel like hearing it. If you could keep those comments to yourself, and not spread them around the office, I think we'll get along just fine."

She looked relieved. "I'm sorry. I shouldn't have said those things. You were right, I'm jealous. I could never date a white man myself, but I admire your courage for marrying one. I wish you all the luck and happiness in the world."

We hugged emotionally and decided to go to lunch together. I knew I had made a new friend. If only all such encounters could end this easily, I thought.

When I got back to the office, I called my mother to find out how she was.

"Better and better," she said. "I'll be off crutches long before the wedding."

"Have you told Greg?"

"No. Your dad and I think you should tell him. He needs to hear it from you, not us."

She was right, of course. I hung up, took a deep breath, and dialed Greg's number.

"Hi, Patty. This is Jasmine. Is Greg there?"

"Hi, Jasmine. He's here, but before I put him on, I'd like to talk to you for a moment."

I felt a sinking sensation in my stomach. How had she found out?

"I want to thank you for lending Greg the money. He's told me everything, even about the other woman, and I've forgiven him. In fact, I've been job hunting and have a few interviews lined up. And Greg's talking to an electronics firm this afternoon about a job. We hope we can pay you back as soon as possible."

So it wasn't about Jeremy! "That's wonderful," I said. "What kind of electronics firm?"

"White owned. Greg's unhappy about it, but I told him he had to compromise. He said if I looked for a job, he would."

"Good for you both." I meant it from the bottom of my heart.

"Jasmine, I'd like to be friends. I know I haven't been the easiest person to deal with, but I think it's time I tried."

"Oh, Patty, of course I want to be friends. I have to admit I didn't like you in the beginning because you didn't work and bossed Greg around too much. But I know I haven't been easy, either. I should have looked past the fact that you didn't have a job. I think that our friendship's long overdue. Goodness, we're family. And I want to tell you, before I tell Greg, that Jeremy and I are going to get married."

"Jasmine!"

The news clearly shocked her, and I waited for a reaction. Finally she said, "I'm thrilled for you. Really happy. I hated not getting a good chance to talk to him at Thanksgiving. And now he's family, too."

"How do you think Greg will react?"

"You know how he is. But I'm on your side, Jasmine. If you need any help as far as the wedding goes, let me know. And maybe we can have lunch next week."

"That would be fine."

"I'll put Greg on."

"Hey, Jasmine, what's up?" my brother asked. He sounded cheerful, more like the old Greg. I was delighted he had worked things out with Patty.

"I'm calling to tell you good news. I got engaged to Jeremy this past weekend. I wanted you to know."

"To *Jeremy*!" he exploded. "I thought you'd have come to your senses by now, but apparently you haven't. How can you even think of marrying a white man?"

"I'm not marrying *a* white man. I'm marrying Jeremy, a man I love with all my heart."

"I forbid it."

"I'm not asking for your consent. How can you act like this, Greg? You're not the same big brother I grew up with, that I respected and looked up to. I don't even know who you are anymore."

"You haven't been through the things I've been

through, little sister. If you had, you'd feel the same way I feel."

"Never. I don't have that much hatred in my body."

"Hatred's easy to learn. But you know, now that I think about it, marrying that white man is a good move. You've bought your ticket. I'm proud of you, li'l sis. You'll never have to work again. He'll pay for everything, and all you'll have to do is keep his bed warm. You're his token, only you don't realize it yet. No white man can love a black woman like a black man can. It's just too bad you'll have to find this out the hard way."

"Go to hell!" I screamed. "I don't even know why I bothered to tell you at all. I used to feel sorry for you, but now I feel sorry for Patty. You're the one with the problem, not her."

"Just don't bring him around," Greg said. "I won't have a white man contaminating my house the way he's contaminated my sister."

"Don't worry. I don't want him within ten miles of you! And as far as the money's concerned, keep it. I don't want it back. Not from you. All I'll do is pray for you, because you need it."

I slammed the phone down with such force I thought I'd broken the receiver. There were tears in my eyes, and I was breathing hard. Why do I let him get to me like this? I asked myself.

The answer was simple. Because he's my brother—and because I love him.

* * *

That night, I told Taylor what had happened. "Boy, do I sympathize with you," she said. "Cameron's run into exactly the same problem."

"I know. It made you break up."

"Break up and come back together. Cameron decided I'm more important than his family. Still, he hasn't asked me to marry him. His brother's never going to change, and he's in real pain. His loyalties are deeply divided. I wish it didn't have to happen to you."

But it has happened, I thought. My brother used to be the most important man in my life. Now someone's come and taken his place, but, oh, how it hurts that I've lost him.

Two days later, my father called. "Do you think you could come over tonight?" he asked, his voice grave.

My heart jumped. "Is it Mom? Anything serious?"

He chuckled. "No. She's fine. She doesn't even know I'm making this call."

"Then could we put it off? I'm trying to work overtime as much as I can so I can make extra money for the wedding."

"I'm afraid it can't wait."

"Then can you tell me what it's about?"

"It's about a talk I had with Greg right after you told him about the marriage."

My heart jumped again. "Okay. Tonight. I'll be there as soon as I can."

* * *

Both my parents met me at the door as soon as I pulled up. They had obviously discussed what they were going to say, and they led me to the patio where Mom had already put out iced tea and a huge salad.

"Greg's terribly upset," my father said.

"I know." I could feel a cold band around my heart.

"He's said that if you marry Jeremy he'll never see you again."

"I knew he was thinking like that. I didn't know he'd say it to you."

"But it affects us," my mother said. "It means no more family Thanksgivings or Christmases."

"Maybe he'll come to change his mind," I said.

"Let's assume he won't. Our family'll be split up."

"I can't believe you're taking his side," I said, suddenly angry.

"We're not taking anybody's side," my father said. "We just want to talk."

"Well, nothing's going to make me give up Jeremy." My voice was cold. I felt betrayed.

"I know that, honey," my mother said.

"And we love you for it," my father added.

"Then why this meeting?"

"Because we're worried, really worried," my father said. "It's not so much that our family will be split, although, of course, that concerns us deeply; it's what'll happen to you. If your own brother feels this way, if he thinks that whites and blacks shouldn't ever be together, that it's 'contamination,' then just imagine how strangers will feel. Just imagine what you'll run into."

"Jeremy and I have talked about that."

"But you've never experienced it. The looks of hatred, the not being able to go to places you might want to visit, the constant prejudice being thrown at you every day."

"We'll stay to ourselves if that happens. We've got each other."

"Each other's not enough in the real world." My father sighed. "Oh, I know how you feel now. Your passion is at its highest, your love at its most explosive. You feel the way about Jeremy that I felt about your mother just *before* we got married. But darling, passion cools and love grows deeper, but more quiet. You've got to be part of the world, you've got to go and have different experiences, make new friends, become a part of society, whether you like it or not. Otherwise, you'll drive yourself crazy in a few years."

"And you'll want children," my mother said. "I know you well enough to know how badly you want them."

I nodded.

"Then think of them. Think of the teasing they'll get in school, think of the fact that they'll belong to neither the black world nor the white. Yes, your love will help sustain them, but in some cases love isn't enough."

Her words hit me like body punches. I felt dizzy, desperate, in despair. To give up Jeremy?

Unthinkable! To live as the people who loved me most in the world described? Unimaginable.

I began to cry.

My mother started to get up, but my father held up his hand to stop her. "Crying'll do her good," he said. "All this is worth crying about.

"It was Greg's call that made us feel this way," he went on. "We realized that his attitude was the world's attitude, that no matter how much you try to deny it and think it doesn't affect you, it *is* the way people feel, the way most everybody feels."

"But you don't," I sobbed. "And Taylor doesn't. Even Patty doesn't."

"Yes, and there are millions like us. But we're still in the minority; alas, there's as much or more hate in this world as there is love. And that's what you've got to face, Jasmine. You and Jeremy both."

"So you advise me not to marry Jeremy?"

"We've thought and thought about it. But Greg's call made it clear."

"You're going to say, 'don't marry'?"

I knew the answer and I thought my heart would break.

"We are."

Chapter Eleven

I DIDN'T STAY much longer. We tried to talk about other matters, but it was impossible. My parents looked at me as though I had some dreaded disease and they did not know how to tell me.

"Look," I said as I was leaving, "Jeremy makes me happy. He's the only man who's ever made me happy. I can't stop that happiness for other people, even for you. I'm tired of living for other people. I'm an adult. It's about time I lived my life the way I want to."

The look on my father's face let me know how distressed he was. In many ways this was as painful for my parents as it was for me.

"I'm sorry," I said. "I'm just confused and frustrated. These should be the happiest days of my life, but they're the most miserable. My brother hates the man I love. My parents don't want me to marry him. Who else doesn't like what I'm doing? Who else wants to live my life for me?"

"Oh, sweetheart," my mother said. "I'm so sorry."

147

She tried to get up, but couldn't and sat back in her chair.

Suddenly, I had to see Jeremy. "Good-bye," I said. "I'll let you know what I decide to do."

I drove to Jeremy's house in a frenzy, my brain refusing to operate in any sensible fashion. Thoughts came and went before I could catch them, and I forced myself to concentrate only on the road, fearful that if I did not, the car would crash.

Jeremy ran to the door as soon as he heard me come in, hugging and kissing me. "Jazz! Darling. What are you doing here?"

At the sound of his voice, I burst into tears.

Later, when I had calmed down, I repeated the entire conversation with my parents. He listened without interrupting, and when I had finished, said nothing, merely walked to the kitchen and returned bringing us both a drink.

"What are you thinking?" I asked.

"Sad thoughts."

"What thoughts? Tell me." I felt desperate.

"That I'm being selfish, that my love for you has blinded me to reality. I wanted you no matter what the consequences. But your parents are right, Jazz, and so are mine—they said to me last night virtually everything your parents said to you. I don't want to deal with people like Ben or your brother, even your parents or mine, every time we turn around."

I felt a wave of fear, as though someone were threatening me with a gun, and my skin grew cold. "Are you saying we're finished? That it's all over?"

"No. I couldn't stand that. I'm saying that maybe

we shouldn't marry in January, that we should go on like this, just as we have."

"If we do that," I said, "maybe we'd never get married."

He thought for a long time before answering. "Maybe we wouldn't. We'd just have to see what happens."

I shook my head. "I don't think I can agree to that," I said. "I want to marry the man I love, and I love you. If we can't marry, then maybe I should look for another man."

He seemed close to tears himself. "The idea of you with someone else—I can't stand it."

"I can't stand it either."

"Then what do we do?"

An idea came to me, I'm not sure how or why. But when it came it seemed the start of an answer. "We go to church," I said.

"To church!" He was astonished.

"Yes."

"I don't think prayer is the answer."

"It's not only prayer I'm looking for." I smiled, suddenly hopeful. "There's something else."

We went to the first service on Sunday morning. By then, my optimism had faded. No matter what happened here, the problems would not go away.

"I hope you're not uncomfortable," I told Jeremy.

"I'm a little nervous," he admitted.

I took his hand and squeezed it. Jeremy's was the only white face among the parishioners, yet there were no hostile looks when he entered, only a buzz of pleasure.

Jeremy heard the choir and was obviously moved by it. The pastor's sermon was on forgiveness. And Jeremy, like all the others, listened with great concentration. The pastor was talking of one man's need to forgive another, but I thought he could have been equally talking about an entire race's need to forgive a different race. And later Jeremy told me he was thinking the same thing.

After the service, I introduced Jeremy to some of the elders and other church members, then, when he was free, to the pastor himself. Jeremy told him how much he appreciated the sermon, and the pastor said how pleased he was to have Jeremy in attendance. "I've heard about you and Jasmine," he said. "I'm very pleased you two are together. Please feel welcome at this church any time, Mr. Collins. We are all one in the sight of God."

Jeremy had a rush assignment, but he drove me home before going back to his house to write. "You see," I said, "we were welcomed in church."

"I was glad of it. But it's an unnatural setting, Jazz. There were probably people there who resented us, only they didn't want to show it in church."

"Most were really glad," I said. "That's what I wanted to show you."

"It's still not reality," he answered. "It's not everyday life. You won't find in church the prejudice that exists in offices and schools."

I knew he was right, and I sat silently, back in the old dilemma. Jeremy dropped me off, kissing me without his usual passion, and I wondered if the problem was already so big that he was losing his love for me.

As soon as I got to my room, I called Simone. "Can I come over?" I asked. "I'm in trouble and need to talk to somebody about it."

"Sure," Simone said. "Danielle's here. We were just about to leave for the beach."

"I'll be right there," I said, and I changed quickly and drove over.

"Thanks for letting me come," I told them.

Simone laughed. "It's good to see you, stranger. It's been hard to get in touch with you lately."

Ever since I had met Jeremy, I had seen little of my friends. Sometimes I missed them; now I was glad they were there for me.

"How are the lovebirds doing?" Danielle asked.

"Not so well." I told them everything. "My heart is torn," I finished. "I don't know what to do."

I expected Danielle to say, I told you so, but instead she came over and gave me a hug. "Oh, sweetie, it is a problem, isn't it?"

"Your father'll come around," Simone said. "If he sees you in a wedding gown, he'll understand that nothing else matters."

"I'm not sure there'll *be* a wedding. That's the point. I should be the happiest woman in the world, but it seems like everybody's against us."

"I think it's more in your mind than real. Just enjoy this time. People are going to say what they say and feel what they feel, no matter who you marry. You can't make everybody happy, only yourself."

"She's right," Danielle said. "It doesn't matter

whether Jeremy's white or black, only that you love him."

I stared at her. "Do you really mean that? I thought you hated that I was going out with a white man."

"I was jealous. Be thankful you have someone like Jeremy to love you. I have no one."

"Why are you jealous? You have more than your share of men chasing after you."

"I need more than men chasing me. That's for sex—I'm good at that, and everybody knows it. But I need a man to love me for me, all of me. Remember when Jeremy was there for you when your mother had the accident? He didn't complain when he took you to the hospital."

I shook my head.

"Well, I need a man like that, to be with me when I'm in trouble as well as in bed."

"As far as your father's concerned," Simone said, "he loves you very much and has every right to feel the way he does. But I think you must listen with your heart to what he's saying. He didn't forbid you to marry Jeremy, now did he?"

"No, I guess he didn't."

"I think he likes Jeremy, but also wants what's best for you. Even if Jeremy were black, he'd still be a little doubtful of the man wanting to marry his daughter. You need to be easier on him, and stop being so hard on everyone else. As far as Greg is concerned, you might as well ignore him. He has his own problems to contend with. Don't let him interfere in your life."

I looked at them both and listened, really listened, to everything they were saying. Here I was ready to believe anything that anybody said about the marriage not working, yet the truth now stared me in the face.

"Maybe I'm the one with the problem."

"What problem?" Danielle asked.

"I think deep down I'm uncomfortable with Jeremy being white. Maybe I wanted him to be black. He's the perfect guy, only he's not perfect because he's white."

Danielle smiled. "I don't think so. You've never dated a white man before, so when you ran into opposition about it, you didn't know how to handle it, and now you blame yourself. Believe me, there's nothing wrong with you. What you need right now is to spend some time alone, away from him, to decide what you really want. You need to be true to yourself. If you really have a problem with Jeremy, not because he's white, but because he's not the right man for you, then break off the engagement."

"I know, Danielle. I know. But I don't want to hurt him."

"By not hurting him, you hurt yourself. It's you who needs protection."

"He's my best friend."

"Sure, but should he be your husband?"

They asked me if I wanted to go with them to the beach, but I felt like being by myself. I drove alone to the marina, got out of the car, and walked toward where the boats were docked. I passed a couple holding hands, laughing and kissing. Both were white. I didn't see any mixed couples at all. Were Taylor and I the only black women in the world going out with white men? I didn't think so, but it sure felt like it.

I had been rushed into the engagement, said yes because I loved the sex and loved the man, but was it really necessary to move so fast? Maybe I should date other men, even make love with other men. Maybe Jeremy could be what I said he was—my best friend—and nothing more.

When I got home, I called Jeremy. "You were right," I said. "Let's not change anything. Let's just keep going on being lovers and friends."

"What's going on?" he asked, sounding suspicious. "What about the woman who wanted marriage or nothing? Have I done something to upset you?"

"It's not you, Jeremy, it's me. I love you, I really do, but there are too many negative things about the relationship."

"Like what?" I could sense his fear.

"I'm just not ready to be in an interracial relationship."

"It's strange," he said. "Now it's I who doesn't want to wait. This is torture. We're torturing each other. Let's decide this minute. Either we get married in January, or we stop seeing each other."

I took a deep breath. "I want you to know that I love you very much, and that I'll always love you."

His voice rose in pain. "So your answer is no?"

"Love me always, too," I cried.

"Oh, I will. I'll always love you. But you don't have

to worry about hearing from me again. I won't call or come by."

"Jeremy, wait," I pleaded, suddenly terrified. It was ending. It was really ending!

"It's better this way," he said. "A clean break." I could hear him stifling a sob. "Take care of yourself and remember, I'll always love you."

There was a click, as though a jail cell door had closed. I had never felt so lost and alone. What had I done? Did I let the best opportunity for happiness I had slip through my fingers? I closed the door so Taylor would not interrupt me, and then I threw myself onto the bed and cried until there were no more tears left.

Chapter Twelve

I SET THE alarm, but when I woke up I felt so terrible I called my supervisor and told her I wouldn't be in to work. Taylor had gone. I lay in my room, staring at the ceiling, fighting the impulse to call Jeremy or to drive over and throw myself into his arms.

At the marina, I thought that when I told Jeremy my decision, I would feel better. I was wrong. I felt worse. I had always felt secure about my decisions in life, but this time, I thought I'd made a terrible mistake. The only chance to get him back was to promise to marry him right away, but I couldn't do that. And besides, he might say no, now that I'd hurt him so badly.

I started to cry again. This was the time Jeremy would have called the office to wish me good morning. I went to fix myself some coffee, then watched some talk shows on television. Everybody had terrible problems, but none seemed as bad as mine.

Around noon, the phone rang. Please let it be Jeremy, I prayed.

"Jasmine, you feeling all right? You were asleep when I left. And now when I called your office, they said you were sick."

"Oh, Taylor, I've really done it this time!"

"What are you talking about?"

"I broke up with Jeremy yesterday."

"I can't believe it. Why?"

"I'll tell you tonight."

"You'll tell me now. I'm coming home."

Thirty minutes later, she walked in. "You didn't have to leave work," I said gratefully.

"Yeah, right. You need me right now, Jasmine, not later tonight. Tell me what happened."

I told her about my conflicts, my decision, my fear, my sadness. "You must understand," I said. "You must have gone through this with Cameron."

"I'm still going through it," she said. "We haven't set a wedding date. He's not even sure he wants to get married."

"How do you *stand* it?"

She sighed. "Because the alternative's worse."

"You mean, not seeing him?"

"Yes."

"Then you think I made a mistake?"

"I think you made an awful mistake. But remember, you're not me, and my opinion doesn't matter. I'm certainly not judging you. I know how hard it is."

"What do you think I should do?"

"Stay as far away from Jeremy as possible. He's in as much pain as you are, and you both need to be alone to think things through. If you come to different conclusions, then nothing you can do, or he can do, can put things right. But if you both want to see each other—or not—then the pain will ease."

"And meanwhile?"

"Go back to life before Jeremy. You were happy enough then. Work as hard as you can, have as much fun as you can, and just glide. Obviously you'll think about him all the time, but try to let things happen naturally. If you and Jeremy were meant to be, then you'll get back together. If not—well, there are thousands of men out there."

"Black men."

"Sure."

"As wonderful as Jeremy?"

"That's for you to find out." She stood up. "Come on. Put on your bathing suit. It's a weekday, and we'll have the beach practically to ourselves."

That evening, I called Simone and Danielle to tell them what I had done. Though I had disregarded their advice, they were both sympathetic. "We'll see more of you," Simone said. "Jeremy's loss is our gain."

"Have you told your parents?" Danielle asked.

"Not yet. I don't want to upset them, one way or the other, until I know exactly what's going to happen."

"What will you say if you show up without Jeremy?"

"That he's working or something. I can hold them off for a few days."

"Even through Christmas?"

Christmas! I hadn't even thought about it. And now I would spend it without Jeremy.

I started to cry.

Two weeks later, Danielle called. "Hey, girl, I've got a great suggestion, and you're not allowed to say no."

"What is it?"

"Simone and I are going to the Catnip Club on Saturday night, and you're coming with us."

"Oh, Danielle, I couldn't. No way."

"I said no wasn't an alternative. You can say, 'What time will you pick me up,' or 'I'll meet you there.' "

It would be good to go out, I thought. Aside from doing some Christmas shopping for my friends and my parents, I had been only at home or in the office, and miserable at both places.

"What time will you pick me up?"

"Atta girl! Eight o'clock. Look dazzling."

I had just about finished dressing when she came to get me. I had decided on a fuschia linen short set. The color would cheer me up, I thought, and show off my legs. Despite everything, I was planning to have a good time.

Danielle was wearing a low-neck dress cut just above her nipples. "I'll just stand up straight all night," she said, laughing, when I commented on it. "Ready to go?"

"Almost. I just need some earrings."

"Well, hurry. Simone's waiting in the car."

I found the perfect earrings, grabbed a purse, scribbled a note to Taylor telling her where I was and asking her to join us if she came home.

The Catnip Club was jumping. There were many more people there than the last time we had gone, and the main room was overheated.

"I don't like it here," I said. "It's too hot."

"Let's hope it gets hotter," Danielle said. "When you've found a man, you won't mind the heat."

"It's not the heat that's bothering her," Simone said. "She's just remembering the last time she was here."

That was true. As soon as I walked in, the vision of Jeremy—what he looked like, smelled like, how he danced—came back in every detail, and I felt a wave of loneliness made more acute because the place was so crowded. The three of us went to the bar and ordered drinks.

"My name's Jimmy," said a voice in my ear. "Want to dance?"

The man at my side was tall and lean. He was wearing jeans and a T-shirt so I could see how muscled his chest was, how thick and strong his arms were. His skin was blacker than mine, and his dark eyes flashed with a smile. Danielle gave a little gasp when he spoke; I could tell how impressed she was.

"What's your name?" he asked.

"Jasmine."

"A beautiful name for a beautiful woman."

I curtsied, smiling. "Thank you, sir." I pretended to be cool, but actually butterflies were flying around inside my stomach. He was gorgeous; he seemed nice; he had a terrific body, but was I ready so soon for another relationship? Why had I come? I wondered, but when he led me to the dance floor and took me in his arms I knew.

He was the best dancer I had ever partnered. Jeremy was good, but Jimmy was superb. I felt light with him, and he could move me with a touch. My body obeyed his commands as though it knew what they would be, and we glided around the floor as if we had rehearsed.

"You dance beautifully," he said.

"It's because of you. I'm usually not this good."

"Looks like we were made for each other." He said the words lightly, but he looked at me sharply, wondering how I would take them.

"Maybe," I said. "Time will tell."

The music had stopped. "Does that mean you'll dance with me again?"

"I'd like a drink while I think about it."

He went off to the bar to get me one. Simone came up to me, laughing. "What is it about you? Every time we come in here, the best-looking man in the place comes on to you."

"I don't know," I said frankly. "I don't think I'm so special."

"And he's black, too! You won't have the same problems."

"Please, Simone. I've only just met him." Her eagerness annoyed me.

"I thought you'd have a good time," she said.

"Here's your drink." Jimmy appeared, carrying a beer and a Coke. "I didn't know which one you wanted, so take your pick."

I chose the Coke and drank it thirstily. I really *was* hot.

The music started again, and Jimmy took my hand. "We don't want to miss a minute, made-for-each-other," he said.

Again I felt light; it was as though he knew me intimately, knew how I liked to move. Briefly, I wondered what it would be like to go to bed with him.

We danced without speaking until the music stopped. Then he led me back to the bar. Danielle and Simone had each found partners, so Jimmy and I were alone.

"Look," he said. "I don't usually act this fast, and I'm really not coming on to you. But I think you're beautiful, you dance marvelously, and I'd really like to go out with you. Do you have a man in your life?"

"Not right now."

I could see his face light up. "How's that possible?"

"I just broke up with a guy."

"His loss is my gain. What about next Saturday? I know a different place, it's really great for dancing."

There was no reason in the world I shouldn't accept. Jimmy was obviously a man I could come to care for, maybe even come to love. I looked at his hopeful face, saw admiration in his eyes. *Say yes*, my brain told me. *Jeremy is out of your life.*

"I couldn't. Please, Jimmy, it's nothing personal. I just couldn't." Suddenly I was crying, huge tears pouring down my face so fast they seemed like a continuous stream. I was dimly aware of Jimmy's surprise as I rushed away from him. The music started again, but I could barely hear it. I searched the dancers for Danielle, and finally found her dancing with a handsome man in the far corner of the floor. She stopped dancing as soon as she saw me.

"What's wrong?"

"I can't stay," I sobbed. "I thought I could, thought I was ready to meet someone else, but I can't."

"Oh," she said. "You got it real bad, don't you?"

"Worse than bad." My voice was a wail. "I love Jeremy with all my heart and soul, and without him I'll never be happy again."

I turned and blindly made my way through the dancers toward the exit. I felt as if I were escaping prison, and I was desperate for fresh air.

A hand gripped my arm. Jimmy, I thought. "*For God's sake*, leave me alone!"

"Never," a blessed voice said. "That's what I've come to tell you."

"Jeremy!"

Yes, it was the man I loved, as though he had answered my silent prayers. Laughing and crying at once, I hugged him so hard we both practically fell down. He kissed my head, my face, my neck, my lips, and I felt I would burn. He smelled wonderful, the familiar mixture of man and cologne, and his body was both hard and soft, known but still mysterious and infinitely desirable.

"Come on," he said. "I know a much better place to make love than out on a dance floor."

Chapter Thirteen

W E DROVE IN our separate cars to his house. As soon as I got out, he was holding me and kissing me, and he could barely open the front door in his excitement. We rushed upstairs to his bedroom, shedding our clothes as we went, as though by delaying we would never be allowed to make love again.

Our lovemaking was passionate and tender, and almost immediately after we had climaxed, we made love again, drawing it out as though we were parts of a meal we wanted to last forever.

Finally, exhausted, happy beyond all measure, letting our fingers trace over each other's body as if to assure ourselves that we were really together again—two become one—we were able to talk.

"How did you find me?"

"Taylor told me where you were. You left a message for her."

"But Taylor never answers my phone, and you don't know her number."

171

"I didn't call her. I came to your house looking for you."

"Why? I thought I had hurt you so badly you'd never want to see me again."

"At first I felt that way. But then I realized that what I feel for you is so special that no problems, no people, no power on earth could keep me away from trying to get you back."

"Oh, Jeremy." I hugged him and gently kissed him. "I felt the same thing. Just tonight. There was this man, this handsome black man, who was attracted to me, I could tell. We danced and it wasn't you. I didn't care who he was or whether he would be better for me, or whether I'd have an easier life with him. All I knew was that he wasn't my Jeremy, and that all I wanted in the *world* was for Jeremy to come back to me—and then there you were."

"I can't live without you," he said simply.

"And I can't live without you."

"No matter what your family thinks? Or Greg thinks?"

"No matter what the world thinks. We'll be all right no matter what happens."

"And our children?"

"We'll help them as best we can. Love makes up for a lot of things, and if we love each other and love them, we'll make them strong."

"Yes," Jeremy said. "I've been thinking. There are so many broken families, black and white. Surely those children have a harder time than ours will, when we're together and have such love."

"I've been thinking of January seventeenth," I said.

"For what?"

"For our official wedding date."

"Why the seventeenth?"

"Why not?"

"Good question. The seventeenth it will be!" He got out of bed, and I watched his superb naked body move to a chest of drawers. He opened the top drawer and took out a small box carefully wrapped in Christmas paper, which he carried back to the bed and handed to me.

"Merry Christmas."

"Oh, Jeremy! I haven't even gotten you a present yet."

"You have time."

"That's right. There are a few days left before Christmas. So why give this to me now?"

"Open it. You'll see."

I tore off the paper. Inside was a box made of velvet, and inside that a ring with a diamond that shone as if it were a star.

Jeremy smiled. "You told me to pick out the engagement ring. I hope you like it."

I tried it on. It fit perfectly. I had never imagined anything so beautiful.

"Well?" he asked, his look telling me that he knew the answer.

"I love it! It's just right. I'm the happiest woman in the whole world."

He pulled away the sheet so that he could look at my body. "And the most beautiful. My Jazz."

"Yes. Yours. For ever and ever."

"And no one will us part."

The next morning I called Danielle and Simone with the news. They were delighted. Danielle told me that before Jeremy showed up at the Catnip Club I looked like a dead fish, for all my lovely clothes. And Simone said that she never doubted for a moment that we would come to our senses. I told them both the wedding date, and they promised to be there.

Taylor wasn't home when I called, but she called me back at Jeremy's that afternoon.

"Oh, honey, that's the best news possible," she said when I told her. "I thought Cameron and I could act as an inspiration to you; now maybe it'll be the other way around. If he goes to your wedding, he'll see that ours is possible."

"Jeremy's family will be there. His parents and his sisters. They're all thrilled for him, or at least they say they are. Anyway, Cameron will see that it's possible for a white family to accept a black woman in their midst."

"I hope so."

I paused. "Honey, you're the best friend anybody could ever have. I don't know how I'd have gotten through this without you."

I could hear her cry. "Jasmine, I love you. And the love of friends is almost as important as the love of a man."

My parents did not know about the fact that

174

Jeremy and I had almost broken up, so when I called them to announce the wedding date, they treated it as routine.

"Just tell me this," said my father. "You're absolutely sure, in your own heart, that this is the man for you?"

Jeremy was standing next to me, and I held the receiver far enough away from my ear so that he could hear, too. "I'm absolutely sure, Dad."

"You've thought it all through? You've heard my warning. You know how tough it will be?"

"We have. And we also know that life isn't worth living without the other in it."

"Then you have my complete blessing," he said. "Mine and your mother's. It'll be tough for us to get used to, but our daughter's happiness is more important than anything else."

"Your daughter's happy. Sublimely, completely, absolutely happy."

I hung up. "And so," said Jeremy, "is her husband-to-be."

Chapter Fourteen

WE DECIDED TO invite only our immediate families, Jeremy's best friend to be best man, and Taylor, Danielle, and Simone as bridesmaids to the ceremony. Afterward, other friends and family members, about sixty in all, would join us at my parents' house for the reception.

Greg refused to come when I called to tell him the date. "I just think it's wrong, Jasmine. You're making a huge mistake, and I don't want to be a party to it."

He was not angry or nasty, just firm.

"If that's the way he feels, so be it," Jeremy said. "I know you're hurt, Jazz, but actually he's hurting himself worse than he's hurting you."

"At least Patty's coming. I think she and I will be really good friends."

"So what's the drill for the wedding day?" he asked.

"I'm going over to my parents' house early. My mom will help me dress. You're not to see me before the ceremony. You just drive over from your house, and we'll meet at the church."

He laughed. "You're the boss. Have you picked a dress?"

"My mom and I are going shopping tomorrow."

"You'd look beautiful in rags."

"The dress won't be rags," I promised.

My boss gave me a day off, and I spent it with my mother, looking for a dress. We found one that we both adored—tight-fitting, low-necked, with satin white roses along the hem and at the shoulders. The price was high, but my mother insisted that I buy it. "It's going to be the most important day of your life," she said. "How do you think you'd feel later if you skimped on it?"

After we got the dress, I picked out rings—elegant gold bands, thick for him, thin for me. I tried mine on below my engagement ring. They matched perfectly.

Christmas came and passed, a festive and happy time. I went with Jeremy to his parents' house, and for the first time met his sisters, who accepted me coolly and cordially. I knew that since they lived far away, I would never get to know them well, but cool and distant was all right with me. At least they were not hostile like Greg.

In January, I began moving my things to Jeremy's house, and actually got used to the drive to work. It would not be so bad, considering that the reward was to share a bed with Jeremy every night. We still planned to go to Cancun for our honeymoon; Jeremy made the reservations and got the plane tickets.

Time passed so quickly that I was barely aware of it. Yet there seemed no rush. I was at peace with myself, happy with my decision.

On the night of January sixteenth, I took my wedding dress and accessories to my parents' house. I would sleep that night in the room I had slept in as a little girl. But in fact, I got very little sleep at all. My mother and I stayed up well past midnight, talking about my childhood, her wedding, how good life was with my father, difficult though he could be. She was off her crutches and able to move freely. "There better be a hostess at your wedding," she said. I felt amazingly close to her, and hoped that my daughter would feel that way about me in some twenty-six years.

In the morning, too excited to stay in bed, I got up and made us all breakfast. We had just finished when the doorbell rang.

"The florist," my mother said. "He's early. Would you get the door, darling?"

I opened the door, expecting a man surrounded by flowers. When I saw who it really was, I gasped. "Greg!"

He was wearing slacks and a shirt open at the throat. His head was down; he could not look me in the eye.

"Come in," I said, wondering what this was all about.

We went to my room and sat on the unmade bed. "I got a job," he said.

"Greg! That's wonderful. Where?"

"With Machin and Roth."

It was a white engineering firm, I knew; one of the largest in the city.

"They have a new policy on open hiring," he said. "I had just the skills they needed. In fact, they couldn't have been nicer. I started there two weeks ago, and so far it's been great."

"You've made this golden day even happier," I told him.

"But I didn't come over just to tell you that."

"What, then?"

"I came to apologize. I've been selfish and pigheaded. I'm prejudiced, I admit it. I thought only about appearances and not at all about you."

I could feel tears come to my eyes. "I've been selfish, too," I said. "I've thought only about how you hurt me, not about how hurt you were yourself and what an incredibly difficult time this must have been for you."

"If you'll let me, I'd like to come to the wedding. To both the ceremony and the reception."

I found to my surprise that additional joy could enter my heart. "Next to Jeremy, you're the man I most want there."

"I love you," he said, "and I want you to be happy forever." He reached into his back pocket, pulled out an envelope, and handed it to me. "This is the money I owe you. You helped me out when no one else would, and I appreciate that."

"You didn't have to pay me back," I said. "You're my brother, and I love you with all my heart. The thing I'm happiest about is that you're coming to the wedding."

He smiled shyly and stood up. "I'd better go get changed," he said. "Don't want to be late for my only sister's wedding."

He rushed away. I don't think he wanted me to see him cry.

My mother helped me dress, then got dressed herself. My father, handsome in striped pants and morning coat, a white carnation in his button hole, drove us to the church, and we were escorted to a little room on the side of the chapel. Soon, my mother left me to take her place in the pews, and I was left with my father, who would lead me down the aisle.

"It's right," he said. "You and Jeremy. Right."

I heard music start, and through the window saw Greg and Patty arrive, then Jeremy's sisters and their husbands, who had shared a car. Jeremy and his parents were nowhere in sight. I guessed that they had arrived before we did.

There was a silence. Then the wedding march began. My father took my arm, and we went to the back of the church where Taylor, Danielle, and Simone were waiting. When they saw us, they preceded us down the aisle, and my father and I followed, walking slowly so I would not step on my train.

The music swelled. I was aware of smiling faces to the left and right of me, and my father's warm and steadying hand. Through my veil, I saw Jeremy waiting for me with the most beautiful smile I could imagine, and I walked toward him—Jeremy, my husband, my love.

Now that you've enjoyed *Shades of Desire*, let
One World / Ballantine's Indigo Love Stories
take you to far away places to hear:

Whispers in the Sand

LaFlorya Gauthier
June '98

Torn between her African lover and her family and
career in America, filmmaker Lorraine Barbette must
decide if she will succumb to wealthy diplomat
Momar's "Whispers in the Sand."

Filled with the sights and sounds of Senegal, this
exotic locale springs to vivid life. The worlds of film
and politics, the powers of love and desire, and one
woman's moment of truth—choosing her career or her
lover—come together in this powerful and captivating
love story.

TURN THE PAGE
FOR A SPECIAL BONUS PREVIEW CHAPTER OF
WHISPERS IN THE SAND

Chapter One

MOMAR DIALLO WAS fuming. He could no longer hold back his resentment. Snarling under his breath, he spoke out. "Damn it, I'm a diplomat, not a diplomatic courier or a diplomatic escort!"

The chauffeur turned around in the front seat of the air-conditioned luxury car. "What, sir?"

"Nothing," Momar snapped, fearing he would explode with anger. The handsome young man turned and glared angrily at the entrance to the Senegalese Embassy. He wondered how much longer he would have to wait. No one in Dakar had told him that at the end of June, Washington, D.C. would be hotter than the capital of Sénégal! He had almost fainted upon arrival the day before when the hot, humid air had struck his face as he stepped outside the airport in Washington. But now his anger was rising to match the soaring temperature. He resented the degradation of this assignment, not to mention the overwhelming arrogance of the foreign minister.

Here he was, having been an ambassador plenipotentiary, with an unblemished service record to more than five countries, sitting in the backseat of an embassy car, waiting to escort a disgraced diplomat home. As the foreign minister had explained, Momar had been given the assignment because he was between postings, he spoke English fluently, and he could be trusted with a confidential assignment. In addition he'd been the one selected to take an emergency diplomatic pouch to Washington.

Some obscure, perverse instinct in Momar made him suspect that it was because he was a griot by birth. The foreign minister was from a so-called superior tribe, and Momar wondered if the man felt that a griot, no matter what his personal accomplishments, would have to obey even when the assignment was beneath him. Momar fumed anew at the memory of the interview. In his current mood of outrage, he was ready to come to any conclusion, look for devious motives in anything.

Now, he was waiting impatiently for Ambassador Lo to personally escort the failed diplomat to his embassy car. The culprit was the reason the Foreign Minister had shown Momar the emergency diplomatic pouch contents.

Momar knew that Omar Sall had been summarily dismissed from his Senegalese diplomatic post for dishonoring it. Sall had been heavily investing money that did not belong to him, and he'd participated in a private American firm of questionable reputation. Sall's diplomatic covering had not made him immune to weakness, greed, stupidity, and bad companions.

"And to think that he was offered that post when everyone knew I was ahead of him for it," Momar murmured, this time too low for the chauffeur to hear him.

The embassy's front door opened, and Momar Diallo sought to control the rage in his mind and heart as he hopped quickly from the big car. He stood beside the chauffeur as the ambassador escorted the disgraced Omar Sall to the car. They were followed by an embassy flunky, who carried the one suitcase Sall was allowed to take with him.

Momar bowed slightly, acknowledging the ambassador's somewhat embarrassed greeting.

"Mr. Diallo, you know that you are not to leave Mr. Sall's side until you are met in Dakar," said the ambassador, a very tall, jet-black, serious Ouloff.

"Yes, sir. I remember my instructions, Mr. Ambassador," he said, standing aside for Sall, an obese man of middle age, who was clad in a white djellaba, white babouches, and no hat. Entering the backseat, Sall seemed more shaken than the day before when Momar had first seen him. Sall's black eyes had the look of a whipped dog as he sat on the far side of the seat, sighing heavily and clasping his hands tightly together.

Having finished giving his instructions, the ambassador turned and reentered the building while the flunky and the chauffeur arranged Sall's suitcase in the front seat of the car.

Momar gladly returned to the car. The heat of the sidewalk had begun to burn his feet through the thin soles of his summer babouches. He had instructions to board the Air Afrique flight to Dakar at the last possible minute in order to attract as little attention as possible. The ambassador was well aware of Sénégal's Radio Tam Tam, and he was concerned that any bad news about a diplomat might adversely affect his own position.

There was maybe one good thing that could come from this hateful mission, Momar told himself. The ambassador had taken him into his confidence; thus, the man might put in a good word for him at the Foreign Ministry back in Dakar. Momar dearly wanted to be posted to the embassy in Washington. Who would not? It was next to the prestige of being posted to the United Nations in New York or to the embassy in Paris, France. He certainly had the seniority and the necessary qualifications, he mused, though it was a long way from his humble origins. As the powerful car sped them toward Washington's Dulles Airport, Momar sat back and recounted his past.

Even though he had finished at the lycée with the highest marks in its history, there was little hope for him to continue his education at that time. His family was from that section of the

Ouloff tribe known as griots. Griots are primarily oral historians, but they also work as artisans. Historically their duties had been to maintain the verbal history of the ruling tribes. They also made the harnesses that the ruling warriors used on their proud Arabian horses. They made the sandals that the warriors wore. They made the scabbards for the warriors' swords and embroidered the finery for the warriors' battle clothing.

Momar was the first of his family to finish at the lycée without knowing how to play the kora or how to recount the history of his traditional tribal masters back to twenty generations and more at weddings, baptisms, and funerals. His family and his circumcision companions considered him an aberration.

The French, who ran the lycée in those days, also considered him a rare bird indeed. Like most Ouloffs, he was tall and thin; but he was always so intense. Most of the time his head was in a book. When school closed the year he graduated, he left Dakar for Casamance to ask his father for guidance about his future. The day after his arrival, the quiet tranquility of their tiny village was turned upside down. A postman from Dakar came looking for him, and all of the villagers were certain that he had committed some terrible crime at the lycée. But they were as dumbfounded as Momar and his family when the postman announced that Momar was to accompany him back to Dakar. He had with him a ticket to Paris! He had been accepted to the Sorbonne!

That night the village threw him a going-away party, during which his family recounted their own history and Momar's accomplishments.

The following morning, Momar set out at dawn in the rattletrap jalopy with the postman.

Until this day, he could not remember a single part of that trip or the plane ride to Paris. It was like a fantastic dream that fades fast upon awakening.

During his years at the university, he could not visit home, even during the summer holidays, because there was not enough money.

After obtaining his master's degree in International Relations, the only place he could think of to apply upon returning home was the Ministry of Foreign Affairs. Because he had learned English very well, thanks to an English girlfriend during those years, Momar's first posting was at the Senegalese Embassy in Monrovia, Liberia. That had been ten years ago.

Since then, he had been posted all over Africa, sometimes in English-speaking countries, sometimes in French-speaking ones.

His most recent posting had been to Zaire. That posting had ended when his Zairian wife had been killed in a car accident. He had asked for and had been granted an immediate leave of absence.

While Momar had long dreamed of a posting to Washington or Paris, he still was not certain that he was psychologically ready. Perhaps, he conceded, the Foreign Minister just might have sent him on this mission to test him. But his mission was so brief that he had seen little of the famous American capital and nothing of New York. What a disappointing waste of his time, he thought as they pulled into Dulles Airport for their shuttle flight to New York.

When Lorraine Barbette boarded the flight to Dakar, she was still smarting from last week's run-in with her now ex-fiancé back in their hometown of Mound Bayou, Mississippi. Tired and disturbed, she had not even protested when the purser had explained that they had overbooked. Apologizing profusely, he'd told them that one of her party of three would have to sit in first class.

Her two colleagues had taken one look at her sad, tired face and nominated her for the honor. She'd nodded distractedly and flopped down. She didn't even react when they teased her about sneaking free champagne back to their crowded section of the plane. Lorraine had simply fastened her seat belt and stared out of the plane's small window. She hadn't even bothered to look around when, seconds before the doors closed for takeoff, two men hastened aboard and took the seats across the aisle from hers.

Not until their flight attendant served champagne and offered her a choice of perfume did Lorraine venture a glance at the last-minute arrivals. Dove gray eyes collided with jet-black ones. The younger man was staring at her with the boldest, yet friendliest and most disturbing deep black eyes she'd ever seen. The look made her throat constrict. Never in her life had she seen eyes so hypnotic. They glinted with crystal reflections. His black face seemed to be carved in ebony planes. It contained an ancient handsomeness that carried the history of his people.

Her glance turned into a stare. His hair had the velvety darkness of a night without moonlight. There was not even a glint in it. Then, his companion, a middle-aged man dressed in a white Senegalese djellaba, said something in a language that Lorraine did not know and the younger man turned toward his seat companion.

Lorraine felt both bewitched and confused. This man's deep ebony eyes disturbed her far more than her ex-fiancé's familiar brown ones ever had.

Momar Diallo fastened his seat belt, stretched his long legs to their full length, and tried to study, his fellow passengers. His eyes always returned, as if of their own volition, to the young, elegantly dressed, tan-skinned woman across the aisle from him. He heard nothing of the takeoff instructions, nor could he remember what Sall had said to him a moment ago, which seemed to anger the older man. Snapping his seat belt around his ample middle, Sall simply stared angrily out the window.

Focusing again on the young woman, Momar decided the girl was a beauty, even if skinny by his standards. Her nose was thin, and her mouth was soft, shapely, if a little sad looking. Her skin color seemed to him like that of honey made from goldenrods. Her hair was thick, jet-black, and she wore it long.

He watched boldly as she put up a well-manicured hand and stroked an errant strand. He wondered what it would feel like to stroke her mane. Long and silky, it would feel sexy, he was sure. She glanced around again, and their gaze locked once more. Her soft gray eyes were long lashed. He sighed.

Momar unsnapped his seat belt and shifted his weight as he accepted the aftershave lotion gift and a soft drink from their cabin attendant.

Why was he so captivated by this girl? He had not been interested in a woman since ... he could not remember. He had not been in love with his wife. Theirs had been an arranged marriage. Yes, it had been a very long time. Too long, he decided. This woman probably would not give him the time of day. She had the look of one of those rich African-American women who sometimes travelled to Africa in search of their roots, inspired, no doubt, by the book of the same name.

Lorraine was bone tired. She closed her eyes and tried not to think; but her mind insisted on replaying that last evening with Andrew in Mound Bayou, a place that had never felt right for her. It was a beautiful, mellow summer night. But Lorraine was sad. She and Andrew should have been on friendlier terms. But ever since she had come home on this visit, he had been touchy and overly sensitive to her remarks. She wondered why he couldn't understand her point of view. Instead, here they were tense and upset, arguing again.

Andrew had done his university and post-graduate work at Ole Miss. Thanks to the civil rights movement, African-Americans were a common sight on the campus these days. He'd returned to Mound Bayou to become the high-school principal. For now he was content, but one day he planned to become mayor. Maybe more, with both Lorraine's family and his own behind him. Lorraine knew she was a valuable acquisition. But though Andrew had a disciplined, organized life, he could be petulant, quick-tempered, and surly.

She could hardly believe it was only last week when they were strolling along and Andrew said that she'd been chosen for this assignment only because of her color. That hurt.

Shocked, Lorraine stopped and cried, glaring into Andrew's face.

"What a rotten thing to say. Can't you accept that I'm the producer and director on this assignment?"

Hoping to diffuse his hostility, she reminded him, "I'd like to think that the years I spent in universities learning French and in my profession are part of it, Andrew. You seem to forget that I've worked for five long years with this company."

"Okay. I agree to that, but I still can't see why you won't set a date for our wedding," Andrew countered stubbornly, this time without the hostility in his voice.

It irked her to think he had such little regard for her ambitions. She resumed walking, Andrew beside her.

She spoke firmly into the ensuing silence, still somewhat peeved. "Andrew, you and I have known each other all our lives. Our families have arranged this marriage. But you seem to want something very different than I do." She stopped, hands on hips, facing him. When he didn't reply, she continued, "You want to be elected mayor. You and I know that unless you marry the bigshot preacher's daughter that won't be possible. I should never have allowed such an arrangement to get this far in the first place."

Andrew was silent.

"Don't you see, Andrew?" she cried. "I need my own career."

"That's your problem," Andrew finally said in a harsh voice.

Lorraine was still attempting to make him understand. "Don't you remember when we were children, how I always dreamed of working in films? So now I've got the chance to do something really exciting. And you don't even care. All you care about is your own ambition!" She had shouted the last sentence. Somewhat sarcastically, she cried, "Marry. Become Mrs. Big Shot Andrew Kemp, the principal's wife, later the mayor's wife, and then what, Andrew?"

It was too dark to see his reaction, so when he

still didn't speak, Lorraine continued, unable to stem her frustration.

"To be frank with you, I was going to call off our engagement anyway. I don't think it's fair to either of us to marry simply to please our families."

She went on as though talking to herself. "Andrew, when I won that scholarship to Concordia University in Montreal and then another to do my graduate work at the University of Montreal, I was in seventh heaven."

"And don't you see, Lorraine, I was in seventh hell," Andrew retorted, his voice on edge again.

"But we saw each other the summers I came home," said Lorraine. "We kept in touch. And you always knew my ambitions. Besides, I never promised I would quit my career and move back to Mound Bayou. I never lied to you. Ever."

She could tell by the stubborn set of his shoulders that Andrew only understood what he wanted to understand. She had tried to prevent an argument with him on this trip, but she realized finally that the engagement was a sham, and Andrew was ready to go through with the sham marriage to further his own ambitions. He couldn't understand why Lorraine would not live a sham life.

Arguing with him, she decided at last, was like trying to unscramble an egg.

With an exasperation she tried to mask, she clamped her well-shaped lips and resignedly stared off into the rural darkness. . . .

"Good morning, ladies and gentlemen. . . ."

Lorraine woke with a start, her right arm slightly numb. She realized suddenly that she was not back home in Mound Bayou but flying high above the Atlantic Ocean. She rubbed her eyes and smoothed her dress over slim legs, which were stretched in front of her seat. Someone had covered her with a blanket during the night. She shook it off and folded it onto the empty seat beside her.

"This is the captain speaking. Breakfast will be served in a few minutes. We are on schedule for our arrival at Dakar-Yoff Airport."

A short time later, they were on the ground. The entire plane had to wait until the young Senegalese man and his older companion were whisked away, as if by magic, to an official-looking black car. Then the passengers and crew were allowed to disembark. Lorraine moved along with her group into the blazing early morning sunshine. "Whew! I wish the captain had mentioned the temperature," she said, wiping her brow with a tissue. Her two male companions had removed their jackets and rolled up the sleeves of their shirts. They were both perspiring profusely. Walking was like wading into an oven.

Ebony porters, airline workers, and customs agents swarmed about in a haze of brilliant local costumes.

Lorraine joined the other passengers and her two colleagues—Sam Benson, their scheduling boss, and Mark Whitman, their cameraman. They waited at the luggage table in front of the customs agent.

"Bonjour, mademoiselle. Avez-vous quelque chose à déclarer?" (Have you anything to declare?) asked a young, jet-black customs agent. He wore a wrinkled khaki safari suit. He eyed her curiously, his marking crayon poised expectantly above her expensive, red leather suitcase.

"Bonjour, monsieur. Non. Je n'ai rien à déclarer." (I have nothing to declare.) Lorraine grinned for the first time since she had left New York. She wiped her olive-colored face with a new tissue and looked around for someplace to discard the other one. The heat was terrible.

The customs agent grinned in response, marked her suitcase, and allowed her to join Sam and Mark.

Got through that all right, she thought with a chuckle, and I haven't used my French regularly since leaving Montreal five years ago!

She was startled when Sam gasped and exclaimed, "Why, Lorraine Barbette, you speak French like a native!"

"Well, not exactly like 'a native,' Sam," she replied dryly, pulling her suitcase from the customs table, "but I do speak it well enough to get by."

Black porters and taxi drivers surged around them, grabbing at their suitcases as they left the customs area, quoting prices and arguing good-naturedly among themselves, confusing the newcomers.

After a few moments, however, a tall, jet-black

man in a white djellaba pushed his way toward them and yelled over the din in English, "Are you the Cultural Sights and Sounds film people?" All three of them nodded, fascinated by the scene unrolling around them.

Already Lorraine knew instinctively, in spite of Andrew's objections, that she had been right to insist on coming to Sénégal. She looked at the airport surroundings and felt, somehow, that this, now and here, was a turning point in her life. Her work meant a lot to her. She had a feeling about this assignment and about this place. Back home she had tried everything she knew to make Andrew understand how much her work meant to her.

"Now," she whispered, close to tears of pure joy, "my first overseas assignment." She felt like hugging herself but instead she followed Sam and Mark into the minivan. They had been escorted to it by the tall black man who had introduced himself as Mansour Diop, explaining that he was to be their guide and chauffeur for the duration of their stay. They shook hands, and he turned on the air-conditioning before he began storing their baggage.

They arrived a few minutes later at the elegant white seaside Hotel N'Gor. Lorraine was swept along with everyone else to the reception desk, where they were assigned their rooms.

Lorraine Barbette was not normally a nervous person, but she was nervous and jittery now. She stroked her long hair. It was a habit she had when she was agitated.

Although she and Micheline Martin had kept in touch by letter, she had not talked with her friend for two years.

Micheline was First Secretary at the Canadian Embassy in Dakar, and they had been friends since their university days in Montreal. But seeing Micheline again was not the reason Lorraine was nervous.

How could she find a way to ask her friend, whom she hadn't seen in years, about the disturbingly suave, handsome Senegalese man she had seen on the Air Afrique flight from New York?

Now here she was prowling her hotel room like a restless panther and trying to find the right words to use when she talked with her longtime friend.

Suddenly, Lorraine picked up the receiver and stabbed the telephone buttons before she lost courage.

"Good morning. The Canadian Embassy," a pleasant voice answered in French.

Lorraine spoke rapidly in the same language. *"Mademoiselle Micheline Martin, s'il vous plaît.* I believe she is your First Secretary."

"One moment, please," the same melodious voice answered briskly.

"Micheline Martin, here. *Bonjour,"* a new female voice said after a moment.

"Micheline? It's Lorraine. Lorraine Barbette,"

the American woman replied, grinning widely for the second time since landing in Dakar. She was picturing her friend's reaction upon learning where she was telephoning from.

"Lorraine, what a clear line we have. You sound so close," Micheline gasped into her telephone.

"I'm in Dakar, at Hotel N'Gor!" Lorraine cried.

Micheline squealed in Lorraine's ear. "I cannot believe it! What are you doing here?"

Lorraine, relaxing by the second, gushed, "I work for this film company. But you already know that. Right?" Without giving her friend more than just enough time to give a sharp exhalation of breath, she rushed on, "Well, I'm here with colleagues to make a documentary film."

"When did you arrive?" Micheline asked breathlessly.

"We got in this morning on the Air Afrique flight from New York," Lorraine explained.

"When can we get together? How long are you going to be here? Did Andrew come with you?"

"Hey, slow down. We'll be here for several weeks at least. Andrew isn't with me." Taking a deep breath, she added, "As a matter of fact, Andrew and I probably won't be seeing each other again any time soon."

There was a short, awkward pause before Micheline carefully replied, "I thought you two would have been married by now."

"When I was visiting Mound Bayou last week on holiday, I told him of my good fortune in getting this assignment, and we had a terrible fight,

Micheline. He was dead set against my coming to Sénégal."

She closed her eyes, reliving the final scenes with Andrew.

"I see," her friend replied soberly. "One of those, eh?"

"Yes." Lorraine sighed.

"I am on my private line, Lorraine, and I am your friend. I sense there is something else you are not telling me, is there not? Will you tell me about it?"

The American woman sighed again. "Is it okay? You're sure?" She swallowed hard. She needed to talk to someone. She and Micheline had often shared their deepest secrets and feelings. Lorraine knew that Micheline was expecting her to talk more about her fight with Andrew, but she really wanted to talk about the mysterious stranger on the plane.

"I . . . I, oh, I don't know how to begin this, Micheline. I flew over with . . . no."

"What on earth are you trying to tell me, Lorraine?" Micheline was lost.

"Oh, I'm all flustered," Lorraine cried. "Well, I saw him on the plane, you see."

"No, I do not see, Lorraine. What are you trying to say? Saw who?" Her friend was totally confused now.

"That's exactly it! Who? There was this Senegalese man in the seat across the aisle from mine, and, and . . ."

"And what, Lorraine?"

"I'm behaving like a moonstruck schoolgirl," Lorraine finished lamely, ashamed of herself.

"And?" Micheline prompted.

"Do you think you might know who he is?" Lorraine began and went on before her friend could utter a word. "I heard the cabin attendant call him *Monsieur* Diallo. And I saw M. D. engraved on his briefcase. He was travelling with a middle-aged man, and both of them left in an important-looking black limo," she finished, laughing a little as she remembered her unabashed spying.

Micheline let out a loud breath. "Lorraine Barbette, that is not at all like you! What has gotten into you? Have you the African fever already?" She began to laugh.

"Aha! You're laughing at me?" Lorraine was sorry she had been so silly. What a stupid-sounding story.

But her friend was already answering her question. "Oh, that would be Momar Diallo."

Now it was Lorraine's turn to laugh and chide her friend. "Do you always know the Senegalese men traveling from New York so well?" she teased.

"No. *Monsieur* Diallo is a very important diplomat, and everyone knows he was sent to Washington to bring back one of their disgraced diplomats. Radio Tam Tam, you know."

"Radio Tam Tam? What's that, a local radio station?" she asked.

"Local gossipmonger, my dear." It was

Micheline's turn to laugh. "A local radio station, indeed!" She could not help laughing again.

"Oh." Lorraine felt disheartened. Why would 'a very important diplomat' even remember having seen her? She was a fool to have mentioned him. Micheline must think she'd lost her mind, she thought.

Micheline returned to the subject of Andrew, already dismissing the conversation about Diallo. "Tell me what happened between you and Andrew," she prompted.

Hesitantly, Lorraine began, "You know he and I have been engaged to marry almost since our childhood. And, well, it was mostly because our two families are so close. They have always wanted the two families joined."

"And with you and Andrew they saw their chance?" Micheline interrupted angrily. "How archaic."

"I know, but that's often how it is with the so-called 'old line' families where I come from," Lorraine answered heavily.

Micheline paused for a moment. "Sounds like here," she said, then asked, "but how do you feel about such an arrangement?"

"To be quite frank with you, Micheline, when Andrew and I were adolescents I though of him as a good and reliable friend. But I really can't say that he ever lit my fire, if you know what I mean." She chuckled. "Marrying him would be comfortable, predictable, stable . . ."

"And dull?" Micheline finished for her.

"You said it. But I always felt I had to marry him because our families took it for granted. His father and mine are co-pastors of our church. His mother and mine control the town's social and cultural life." How stupid it all sounded now, but she went on. "They expect him to be mayor one day, if we marry. Oh, it all sounds so cut-and-dried, doesn't it, Micheline?"

"Try and forget about all that now that you are in Sénégal. Try to enjoy your time here. Which reminds me, will you be coming to the reception at the Foreign Ministry tonight?" Micheline asked.

Lorraine brightened. "It's in our honor, my dear," she chirped. "Oh, Micheline, I'm so excited about that. It's certainly the first time I've ever been to a reception where I was one of the persons being honored. It sounds so, so . . . important!" she gushed.

"It is important," Micheline replied, laughing. "See you tonight then. And, Lorraine, I sincerely thank you for telephoning. It is simply great to hear from you again," she finished warmly.

"Same here," Lorraine replied, just as warmly. She felt much better now.

They both rang off.

By the time their car had reached the Foreign Ministry building, Momar's anger and frustration had solidified into a hard lump in his chest. He watched as Sall was led away, where to, Momar did not know, nor did he care.

207

An hour later, just as he was congratulating himself on an unpleasant job well done and was almost out the door, the Foreign Minister's secretary halted him. Momar knew he should have been suspicious when the minister, a short, thin Toucouleur, waved him into his office with a big smile. Momar had been caught off guard.

After both men were seated, the minister asked him about his trip, in detail. Then he gave him the highlights of the ambassador's written report and offered him tea.

Certain now that he was about to be named to a post in the United States, France, or England, Momar relaxed and sipped his tea. Why else would the Foreign Minister get so cozy? Momar asked himself.

"Diallo," the minister said between loud sips of tea.

Here we go! he thought. I have got my posting!

"Er, Diallo," the minister was going on, "you handled this assignment so well that we have something else for you," he concluded expansively.

I do not like the sound of that "something else," Momar thought. He tensed, waiting.

Without further preamble the minister let him have it: "There is a film crew just arrived in Dakar from America. They already have a guide and chauffeur, Mansour Diop, from the Ministry of Information, but I must assign a diplomatic escort from this office. And, since you speak English, you are our man! Ahem." The minister took another loud sip of his tea.

Momar almost spilled his. Another escort assignment! He almost screamed aloud.

Instead he choked out, "Ah, aah, *Monsieur le Ministre . . .*"

"I told the Minister of Information we could count on you, Diallo!" the minister said happily, reaching over the small, low table to vigorously shake Momar's hand.

"Your duties as the escort are limited. They will only need you weeks from now to smooth the waters in Ziguinchor. Their guide, Diop, will take care of them in the bigger cities," the Foreign Minister said, trying to appease Momar.

"By the time this assignment is over, I know for sure, an important post will be available for you. Go to the Ministry of Information tomorrow afternoon. They will give you more particulars," the minister finished in a dismissive tone. Momar knew the interview was over and there was no need to protest. But his mind viciously did: There is a post available *now* in New York, and in Washington, and in Paris, and in London!

Momar wanted to cry. Not only was he an escort again but he had been lent to another ministry! *Zut!* Damn! He fumed silently, all the while smiling weakly as the minister escorted him to the door. At least he was finally free to go home.

For the first time in a long time, however, home held no thrill for him. But he was tired and weary. Also, he could not forget the young woman he had seen on the plane.

"And, yes, damn it," he said to the sidewalk,

"here I go escorting someone else. This time a whole crew of Americans! Allah save me." He stalked to where his car was parked, jerked open the door, and threw his carry-on bag and briefcase into the backseat. Both landed with a heavy thud. The briefcase tipped and fell to the floor. He never even noticed.

After angrily scrunching behind the steering wheel, Momar slammed the car door shut. He turned on the ignition and stomped on the gas to start his car. It jerked, as if it, too, were angry, then stopped dead. More carefully Momar eased the car from the parking lot and into traffic.

"I will bet those damned Americans are like that last bunch who went around trying to photograph the girls in the countryside who went bare chested," he spat, talking to the car.

All they were interested in was looking for something that would be sensational back in America. What a mess, escorting an ignorant American film crew! "Momar, how low can you get?" he asked himself.

When she put the telephone down, Lorraine headed for the bathroom. The short talk with her friend had helped her morale a lot.

"Wow! Am I in Africa, or what?" she exclaimed, relegating Andrew to the back of her mind. But she could not do the same with the handsome diplomat she had seen on the plane. She literally glided to the bathroom. Pale orange and sand-colored hand-painted tiles covered the walls and floor.

"I could swim in that tub," she cried, staring at the biggest bathtub she had ever seen. One whole wall was a mirror and she stared at herself and laughed out loud. She was rumpled, her thick black hair was out of place, her lipstick was smeared, but her dove gray eyes glowed with delight as she turned the bathtub faucet to warm and added perfumed oil to the water.

A few minutes later she sighed contentedly as she lowered herself into the water richly perfumed with Chanel No. 19 bath oil. She was shocked to find that, reclining, her toes did not touch the end of the tub even though she was tall enough to be a fashion model. Nevertheless, she submerged herself up to her neck, careful not to slide beneath the water.

She sighed again. "This is Africa! This is Sénégal! And this is where that *Monsieur* Momar Diallo lives! Whoopee!" She felt like a schoolgirl. She savored his name, recalling every detail of his face and his warm, brooding eyes. They had made her feel as though she had changed planets, not just countries and continents.

Much later, Lorraine turned on the bedside radio. The room was flooded immediately with an African song. She did not understand the words, but the song itself had a haunting quality to it. She recognized the dreamy sound of the kora, the guitar-like instrument she had once seen played when Les Ballets Africains had given a concert in

New York. She listened a few minutes, her chin propped in her hands, then she turned the volume down, stretched luxuriously again, and was soon asleep.

Love Letters

Ballantine romances are on the Web!

Read about your favorite Ballantine authors and upcoming books on our Web site, LOVE LETTERS, at **www.randomhouse.com/BB/loveletters**, including:

♥What's new in the stores
♥Previews of upcoming books
♥In-depth interviews with romance authors and
  publishing insiders
♥Sample chapters from new romances
♥And more . . .

Want to keep in touch? To subscribe to Love Notes, the monthly what's-new update for the Love Letters Web site, send an e-mail message to
loveletters@cruises.randomhouse.com
with "subscribe" as the subject of the message. You will receive a monthly announcement of the latest news and features on our site.

So follow your heart and visit us at
www.randomhouse.com/BB/loveletters!